MW00944113

BADGER THURSTON and the Mud Pits

BY
GUS BRACKETT

ILLUSTRATIONS BY
DON GILL

Twelve Baskets Book Publishing
Three Creek, Idaho

Twelve Baskets Book Publishing, LLC
48600 Cherry Creek Rd.
Rogerson ID 83302
www.12bookbaskets.com
gus@12bookbaskets.com

ISBN 978-0-9841876-3-8

Other books in this series:
Badger Thurston and the Cattle Drive
Badger Thurston and the Runaway Stagecoach

Table of Contents

Chapter 1	1
Chapter 2	17
Chapter 3	31
Chapter 4	47
Chapter 5	59
Chapter 6	69
Chapter 7	81
Chapter 8	91
Glossary	109
From the author	113
About the author	115

Illustrations

Map	
Illustration 1	9
Illustration 2	18
Illustration 3	36
Illustration 4	53
Illustration 5	66
Illustration 6	74
Illustration 7	88
Illustration 8	99

Map

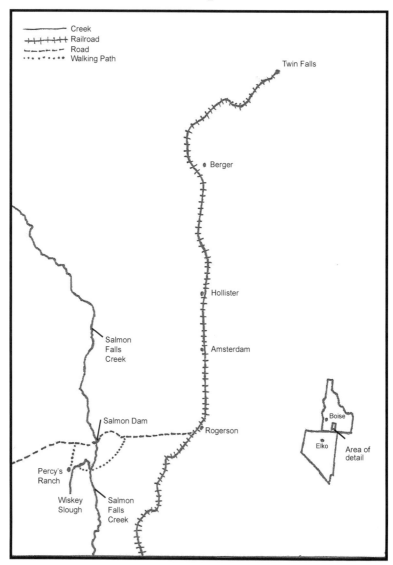

Creek
Railroad
Road
Walking Path

Twin Falls

Berger

Hollister

Amsterdam

Salmon
Falls
Creek

Salmon Dam

Rogerson

Percy's
Ranch

Wiskey
Slough

Salmon
Falls
Creek

Boise

Elko

Area of
detail

Chapter One

BADGER SWINGS HIS TEN-POUND sledgehammer high above his head and slams it onto a steel chisel—*ping!* The sun glares off the rocky ledge where Badger works. The teen swings his hammer again—ping! The chisel looks like a giant nail sinking into the black rock.

As Badger raises the hammer, he hears someone shout from above, "Fire in the hole!"

"Fire in the hole!" several workers echo throughout the worksite.

Fire in the hole, Badger thinks. *That's what dynamiters yell when they light the dynamite!*

Badger drops his hammer and runs. In six steps, he reaches the twenty-five-foot ladder and begins scurrying up the canyon side.

"Get out of there, Badger!" a man yells from above him. "You are too close to the dynamite!"

Badger grabs the next ladder rung and yanks himself up.

"Hurry up!" the accented voice shouts. "Only fifteen seconds are left on the fuse!"

Badger climbs faster, but his foot slips off the rung. Badger holds on with both hands and thrashes around for the step with his foot. His boot toe finds a rung and he scurries upward again.

Twelve ... Eleven ... Ten, Badger thinks, counting down the time.

As Badger's head reaches the rocky clifftop, a tanned hand grabs his shoulder. The giant hand squeezes, and Eliyah hoists Badger up the remaining rungs and over the canyon rim.

"Run, Badger!" he roars.

Terror fills Badger's eyes as Eliyah claps his small brown derby hat to his head and churns his tree-trunk-thick legs like a loping mule, half dragging a sputtering Badger behind him.

The clock in Badger's head counts down as they run. *Three ... Two ... One ... KABOOM!* The massive builder throws Badger to the ground and dives on top of the winded teen. Badger gasps for air as Eliyah shields him from the blast. Badger feels the warm shock from the blast, and then small rocks rain down from above. Eliyah groans in pain as the hot rocks shower him, but Badger is completely protected. The rocks stop falling, and Eliyah stands up. A cloud of dust falls to the earth and covers Eliyah and Badger with a brown powder. Eliyah reaches down and pulls Badger to his feet.

"That was a close one," Eliyah says. "Too

close for me." Eliyah speaks clearly but has a thick Bulgarian accent. His voice is raspy like a frog and deep enough to sing bass in the choir.

"That blast could've cooked me," Badger says as he brushes the dust off his blue jeans. "I know I'm new here, but shouldn't somebody tell me before they light the dynamite?"

"Nikos and the other Greeks are in charge of the dynamite," Eliyah explains. "They do not like us Bulgarians and want us to leave. They sometimes set the dynamite without clearing the site."

"But I'm not Bulgarian," Badger says.

"Maybe you are working too close to me," Eliyah says with a half grin. "I think they are trying to hurt me."

Badger's not sure if Eliyah is joking. Eliyah is always laughing with the men, but he rarely jokes about safety.

Badger removes his hat and shakes the powdery dust off it. He checks his brown denim coat for any new holes. Badger looks up and sees several cuts on the big builder's arms and back.
"You're bleedin', Eliyah. You need to report your injuries to the foreman."

Eliyah laughs like a growling bear. "Badger, Badger, Badger, you cannot make sausage without killing a pig, and you cannot build the biggest dam in the world without a few cuts and bruises."

"But we need to report the accident," Badger says. "Those cuts need cleanin'."

"I would rather bleed to death than tell Win Churchman anything," Eliyah says, his dark eyes

3

trained on the husky teen. "Do not worry, Badger. We Bulgarians can take care of ourselves. Always have; always will."

THE SUN PERCHES above Badger's left shoulder. The winter day is frigid, but Badger sweats from the hard work. Salmon Dam is nestled in a narrow canyon. Below the dam is a steep-sided rock canyon. The dry creek bed lies nearly two hundred feet below the canyon rim. Upstream from the dam, a wide valley holds the backwaters. The concrete dam is nearly two hundred feet wide at the bottom. The dam arches against the rising water behind it. The concrete tapers to the top and forms a neat, narrow pathway across the top. Only one gigantic segment remains unfinished, an eighty-foot section on the dam's east side. A solid wooden frame holds the drying concrete, or mud, the workers poured today. Another set of wooden forms climbs higher, awaiting tomorrow's concrete.

Badger swings his sledgehammer above his head and slams it down on his chisel, like a hammer hitting a nail. Badger is operating a single jack. He holds the chisel himself and hits it with his hammer. The crews are drilling one-inch holes into the rock where they will place dynamite to blow the rock off the canyon wall. This is creating a flat edge to pour concrete against, which will seal the enormous dam. Again and again, Badger strikes the chisel with his hammer, turns the chisel a quarter turn, and strikes it again.

Badger's arms and back ache, and he

4

breathes deeply with every swing. His feet hurt, and his glove-covered hands are raw. But the young cowboy hired on for this project, so he works hard at his grueling task.

"Lawrence Thurston, Eliyah Dobrev— foreman's office!" a man in the distance yells.

"Lawrence Thurston, Eliyah Dobrev— foreman's office!" several men echo so everyone in the worksite can hear the message.

Badger cringes as he hears his real name echoed through the worksite. Badger sets down the tools and steps to a rope ladder. He climbs its rickety wooden rungs up the rock face and then hikes the short distance to his destination.
The foreman's office is a simple structure. If it were a house, it would be small enough to call a shack. It has one door with windows on either side. Its roof is shingled, but the wood-sided building isn't painted. Badger rolls his shoulders and twists his head from side to side to relieve the tightness in his muscles. Eliyah arrives within moments. He nods to Badger, opens the door, and the two stroll through the doorway.

Inside, a small man sits behind a desk. Mr. Churchman wears a bright red shirt and baggy overalls. His brown hair is turning gray, and he has worry wrinkles around his green eyes. He wears a brown hat that has a small three-inch brim and low crown. It looks like every other brown hat except for two small holes worn through the crown where he always grabs his hat to put it on or take it off.

Three lanterns and two candles light a series

of blueprints, journals, and ledgers scattered across the desk the foreman sits behind. Mr. Churchman stares intently at his work, ignoring Badger and Eliyah. He looks at a drawing of the dam design, finishes a calculation in his notebook, and drops his pencil to the desk. Only then does he look up at the pair.

Mr. Churchman scowls. "I hear there was an accident today."

"We had a close call but no accident," Eliyah says with a nod and smile.

"I hear you two got pelted with rocks from a dynamite blast," Mr. Churchman says.

"My men and I drill holes and pour concrete," Eliyah says. "Nikos and the Greeks set charges and light dynamite."

"But it is your job to get your men out before it goes off," Mr. Churchman says. "Any injuries to you or your crew are your responsibility."

"Yes, but there were no injuries," Eliyah says.

"I could fire you for not reporting an accident."

"Mr. Churchman, I am the only Bulgarian who speaks English. Without me, you would lose a quarter of the crew."

"I think this dam would get built faster without you lazy pigs."

Badger looks at his boots. Mr. Churchman's words make Badger's skin squirm. With comments like this, the young worker understands why nobody likes the foreman. Badger feels invisible as the discussion gets hotter than a grease fire.

"Well, pigs like mud, and mud makes dams. We are, how do you say, the best pigs for your mud."

Mr. Churchman swallows his next words and stares daggers at Eliyah. He looks like an overfilled balloon that's about to pop.

"This morning's blast uncovered a den of rattlesnakes. You and the boy, go clean them out. That should give you time to think about worksite safety."

"The man who pays the piper picks the tune," Eliyah says.

"What are you talking about?" Mr. Churchman asks.

"You are the boss," Eliyah says with a tight smile and shallow bow.

Badger and Eliyah spin and stride out the door.

"This job would be a lot better if Win Churchman would disappear," Eliyah says louder than Badger is comfortable hearing.

"Whattaya mean?" Badger asks.

"Just what I said." Eliyah halts and turns toward Badger. "If Win Churchman were to fall into wet concrete, I would not pull him out or say a word until the mud was hard."

"You can't mean that," Badger says to his crew boss. "And if you do mean it, you can't talk about it. Somebody might hear."

"Everyone in this camp already knows," Eliyah says with a laugh. "If anything were to happen to Win Churchman, the search for the guilty person would start and end with me. But I will not do anything. Without me, all the Bulgarians would be out of work. I cannot do that to my men."

Badger nods. He doesn't like Mr. Churchman; nobody likes Mr. Churchman. But Badger doesn't want anything to happen to the foreman or Eliyah.

THE BRIGHT SUNSHINE LIES about how cold the day is. Badger pulls up his blue scarf so it covers his ears. To keep his legs warm, the young worker wears two pairs of pants and two pairs of socks under his cowboy boots. January in the high desert is always cold, but Badger is annoyed that even sunshine doesn't cut the chill. He is also annoyed that Eliyah looks as happy as a kid in a candy store as he works in the cold—in a snake pit.

Living rattlesnakes are deadly poisonous, so Badger and Eliyah work cautiously. Even with gloves on, Badger is afraid to touch the listless serpents. He tries to lift them out of the pit with a shovel, but they slither off every time. He tries to impale them with a stick, but the lethargic creatures wiggle off. Every time a snake moves, Badger jumps like a frightened child and screams.

"This isn't workin'," Badger complains. "How are we gonna get 'em out?"

"How about you climb in and throw them up to me?" Eliyah asks without his normal smile.

Badger's jaw drops. "What if they wake up? What if I can't get back out? You don't really expect me to crawl down there, do you?"

Eliyah laughs. "I was just joking, Badger. You should have seen your face though. I thought you were going to be sick."

After about an hour of struggling, Badger

and Eliyah have perfected a technique for removing the mostly motionless reptiles. Badger uses a post-hole digger, a tool that looks like two shovels tied together with a hinge. It is designed to dig dirt from the bottom of a deep, narrow hole. Badger reaches into the pit with the post-hole digger and squeezes the snakes. He lifts the snakes out like a bird picking up a bunch of worms and places them in a large bathtub.

The explosion killed most of the snakes, but some wake when Badger pulls them out. When one squirms to life, the young cowboy uses the post-hole digger to chop it into pieces. Snakes move slowly in the cold, so Badger is in no danger. But his nerves scream every time one moves.

Each time Badger fills a steel bathtub with serpents, Eliyah carries the tub to the back side of the dam and dumps the snakes into the water. By the time Eliyah returns with the empty bathtub, Badger has nearly filled a second tub with scoops of rattlesnakes.

"The fish will feast tonight," a grinning Eliyah says. Badger likes the way Eliyah says *feesh*.

Badger dumps another shovelful of snakes into the tub. One moves, so Badger whacks it with his post-hole digger. Eliyah picks up the tub and smiles.

"Eliyah, why are you smilin'? This is the worst job Mr. Churchman could think to give us."

"In Bulgaria, we say, 'Whoever has a cow drinks milk.' You should be happy to have a job. A job is a job. I do my job with a smile, and it is a good job. You do your job with a frown, and it is a bad job. All you need is a smile for this to be a good job."

Badger cracks a narrow grin. Eliyah has a way of explaining life that is so simple. His truths are hard to argue. For the short time Badger has known the big Bulgarian, he has liked the older man. That's not surprising since everyone likes Eliyah—except the camp workers who don't like any Bulgarians. Badger laughs as he picks up a shovelful of snakes like a child fumbling with a spoonful of spaghetti. Eliyah grabs the full tub and carries it toward the canyon's edge.

Badger starts filling the empty tub. He reaches into the pit and pulls up a bundle of snakes. One moves, but with Badger's improved attitude, he laughs instead of flinching. He smacks the slow-moving snake and reaches in again.

Badger works methodically. The tub is nearly full, but Eliyah hasn't returned yet. Badger looks around. It is a short walk to the canyon's edge; Eliyah should be back by now. Badger jogs toward the back side of the dam. As Badger approaches, he sees a gigantic silhouette. Eliyah is motionless as he stares at the nearly completed dam.

"Eliyah, are you all right?" Badger asks as he slinks to the canyon's edge.

Badger's question startles Eliyah. The crew leader looks at Badger and then down at the freshly poured concrete. Badger peers at the structure's new eighty-foot-long by fifteen-foot-wide section of concrete near the top of the dam. A temporary wooden form holds the wet mud in place. Badger sees a depression in the hardening concrete and a hat lying on top.

"What's goin' on?" Badger asks.
Eliyah nods toward the concrete. "I just noticed a hat down there."

"Did someone lose a hat over the edge?" Badger asks.

"I do not think anyone lost his hat. It looks more like he lost his balance. A hat would not disturb the concrete that much."

Badger looks again and notices that the hat looks just like Mr. Churchman's. Badger remembers what Eliyah said about Mr. Churchman falling in concrete.

"Man down! Man down!" a voice cries out. Workers echo the cry, and it grows weaker to Badger's ears as it is repeated farther away. A crowd gathers at the top of the canyon. Ropes are thrown over the edge, and workers scurry past Badger and Eliyah to climb down into the fresh mud. The men stand waist-deep in the concrete and poke through the mud with shovel handles they grabbed from a nearby platform.

Badger and Eliyah stand as still as statues as they watch the search. They don't speak. They stare blankly at the commotion on the dam as the workers frantically search for the hat's owner. More than forty men stab through the concrete, but all they find is concrete. Despite the mud sloshing around in the forms, the concrete slowly hardens. After thirty minutes of searching, the first man gives up and climbs up the rope. One by one, the men shrug their shoulders with disappointment and climb out of the mud pit.

The last man climbing up the rope looks at Eliyah and says, "Whoever is down there is dead. You can't be in mud for that long without breathin'."

"Who is it?" another man asks. "Did anyone see who fell?"

"Who yelled 'man down'?" asks Mr. Schmitz, the project engineer.

"I did," a stocky young man named Nikos says. "I yelled 'man down' when I saw Eliyah push Mr. Churchman into the pit."

Eliyah gasps and glances around the ledge like a puppy that just peed on the floor. Nikos marches to Mr. Schmitz with clenched fists. His muscles bulge, and he looks like he is carrying two watermelons under his arms. He has olive skin and thick, black hair. His thick eyebrows are always furrowed like he's angry, and he talks with an accent similar to Eliyah's but distinctively different. Eliyah shakes his head, looking at the ground. Badger's head swivels back and forth between the searchers and the giant Bulgarian.

"Eliyah, you didn't push him in, did you?" Badger asks.

"Did you see what happened, Eliyah?" Mr. Schmitz asks.

The massive builder looks directly at Mr. Schmitz but says nothing.

"Did you see anything?" Mr. Schmitz asks,

this time louder than necessary.

"That is Mr. Churchman's hat," Eliyah says as he lifts his hat and wipes sweat from his thinning hair.

"What happened to Mr. Churchman?" Mr. Schmitz asks.

"I do not know," Eliyah says.

"What–happened–to–Mr.–Churchman?" Mr. Schmitz says, speaking every word clearly.

"I do not know," Eliyah repeats almost in a stupor. "I do not know. I do not know."

Badger worries for his friend.

"Did you push Mr. Churchman over the edge?" Mr. Schmitz asks.

"I do not know," Eliyah says.

"I didn't see anybody fall," Badger says. "So both of you were here," Mr. Schmitz says, "but neither of you know anything."

Eliyah and Badger are silent.

Mr. Schmitz rolls his eyes. "Well, since both of you are not talking, we will lock both of you in the gatehouse and let the sheriff figure out who killed Win Churchman."

"My men and I will take these two murderers to the gatehouse," Nikos says. "Wait a minute," Badger pleads. "I wasn't even here!"

Nikos moves close to Badger and whispers, "You are just like the Bulgarians. You cannot shut up. Listen close, cowboy. Keep your mouth shut— or you might be the next one over the edge."

Two men grab Badger's arms. The teen

looks behind him to see Nikos and another man gripping Eliyah. The builder's head is bowed, and he mumbles, "I do not know," over and over again.

Chapter Two

THE GATEHOUSE IS a square building that has a roof like an Egyptian pyramid. It is not a jail, but it has the feel of a jail. The concrete structure has a steel door, and bars cover its three windows. It doesn't have a chimney or heat stove. A shiny, new padlock on the door keeps people out. But in this instance, the lock is keeping Badger and Eliyah in. Badger huddles in one corner. The sun is down, and the camp is ready to sleep. The evening chill cuts through Badger, and he focuses his energy on not shivering. His brown cowboy boots offer little protection to his numb toes. He wears thin leather gloves, and his hands are so cold, they hurt.

Eliyah refuses to sit. He fidgets nervously in a corner of the single-room building. The room has no furniture and only one fixture—a giant wheel on an axle that sticks up from a four-foot-long by four-foot-wide hole in the ground. When turned, the wheel opens or closes a gate below it so water can flow through the tunnel to a canal. The gatehouse's purpose is to protect the gate and wheel from the weather.

Badger and Eliyah expect to wait at least through the night. Sheriff Jones, the county sheriff, is stationed in Twin Falls, more than an hour's train ride away. As the temperature drops, the cold bites deeply into the pair.

Badger is annoyed. He didn't see what happened. His only mistake was being at the wrong place at the wrong time, just like when he had to dodge rustlers on a cattle drive. Badger saw Mr. Churchman's hat, but he can't believe someone as nice as Eliyah could kill anyone.

"Eliyah, do you know what's goin' on?" Badger asks.

"I really do not know," Eliyah says.

Badger rolls his eyes. *This is the same "I do not know" song Eliyah has been singin' since this nightmare started,* he thinks.

"No, Badger. That is the problem," Eliyah says with emphasis. "I do not know what happened. I walked the snakes to the canyon rim. As I was dumping them, I heard something fall into the mud. I put down the tub, turned around, and saw someone running away. When I looked over the edge, I saw Mr. Churchman's hat."

Badger shakes his head. Eliyah is as solemn as a high school principal doling out punishment. "This is why I left Bulgaria. The police would enter our churches and arrest anyone they wanted to. We would be put in jail and beaten until we confessed to crimes we did not commit." A tear wells up in Eliyah's eye. "I never did anything wrong, but they would hit me and kick me and starve me until I confessed. So I came to America. But here I am, again accused of something I did not do. ... I have nowhere else to go."

Badger sits in silence. He has known Eliyah for only a few weeks, but he really likes the gentle giant. He still isn't sure whether Eliyah pushed in Mr. Churchman, and he is still annoyed that he got dragged into this mess.

"Why didn't you yell 'man down'?" Badger asks.

"Well, I told a lot of people this afternoon that I would not pull Win Churchman out of drying cement. When Nikos accused me, what could I say?"

"Did you push him in?"

"No, no, I could not!" Eliyah says forcefully. "I cannot get angry enough to murder."

I want to believe Eliyah, Badger thinks, but everyone in the camp seems to think Eliyah did it— or I did it.

"Do you think Nikos did it?" Badger asks. "He threatened to toss me in the mud if I didn't keep quiet."

"Maybe, but I doubt it," Eliyah says. "He wants me dead, not Win Churchman."

"Why does Nikos hate you?"

"I am still here," Eliyah says. "Nikos has a village of men in Greece waiting for jobs in America. Without me to translate, my men could not take orders and could not work here—"

"And Nikos could fill all those jobs with men from his village," Badger finishes.

"If I were dead, then I would guess Nikos was the murderer," Eliyah says. "But why would he kill Win Churchman? He needs Mr. Churchman to hire the men from his village."

"Do you know who was runnin' away?" Badger asks.

"I do not know," Eliyah says. Badger instinctively rolls his eyes at another *I do not know.*

"Well, what did he look like?"

"He was not big or tall—maybe your size; maybe a little bigger. He had brown pants and a brown coat."

"Could you see his face?" Badger asks. "What kinda hat was he wearin'?"

"He was running away, so I could not see his face, and his head was bare."

"What color was his hair?" Badger asks.

"I could not really tell. … His hair was thin and maybe a little gray," Eliyah says.

Badger turns his back to his friend. *Eliyah is right,* he thinks. *He really doesn't know anythin'.*

"We'll have to figure out who was runnin' away," Badger says. "He might have some answers to straighten out this mess."

Eliyah nods. He grabs the bars covering a window. The gatehouse is by far the sturdiest building in a camp full of shacks.

"We will not find out anything stuck in the gatehouse," Eliyah says, "and we could freeze to death once full night sets in."

"Whattaya have in mind?" Badger asks.

"I play cards with the miners who are

tunneling underneath here," Eliyah says as he looks down the large hole where the gate stands. "They think they are close to breaking through the rock to the outside. The tunnel is supposed to come out of a hill about one hundred yards below the dam, about where they are building the canal. If we drill into the tunnel, we might be able to get out. If not, we can at least stay warm trying."

Eliyah enters the hole. Badger looks in but can't see the bottom. Eliyah climbs down and then hangs from the wheel like an ape. The builder lets go and drops into nothingness. Badger chokes on a gasp as he hears Eliyah hit the ground.

"Come on down, Badger," Eliyah yells from below.

"How far is it?" Badger asks as he strains his eyes to see the rocky floor.

Badger hears a flint striking and then sees a little flame dancing. Eliyah touches the flame to a candle, and the flame throws enough light for Badger to see. The drop is less than ten feet, so Badger hurries into the hole, hangs from the gate wheel, and drops to the floor.
Eliyah is holding a candle the miners left in the tunnel. The candle has a carrying hook and a spiked end, which is designed to fit into holes drilled into the rock.

Eliyah and Badger stride down the tunnel, which is tall enough for the giant Eliyah to stand in without crouching. When the dam is finished, this not-yet-completed tunnel will flow with water heading to the canal system that will irrigate 78,000 acres of desert farmland. The crews will need to hurry to complete the project before the spring planting season. That is why everyone is hurrying—carpenters, miners, dynamiters, excavators, and a whole crew of flunkies doing odd jobs around the worksite.

BADGER'S EYES ADJUST TO the dark and then readjust every time the candle flickers. *I wonder whether the candle really helps,* Badger thinks. Then he looks behind them into the deep, black nothingness of the dark tunnel. Eliyah stops suddenly. With his eyes behind them, Badger blunders into Eliyah's back and bounces off the behemoth man like he hit a canyon wall. Eliyah eyeballs Badger on the ground.

"There is no time for resting," Eliyah says with a chuckle. Badger shakes his head and rolls his eyes.

Badger stands up and squints. He sees craggy rock in front of them, which means they've reached the end of the tunnel. Eliyah moves the candle along the wall, searching for something. Badger isn't sure what. Finally, Eliyah locates a hole chiseled into the wall. He places the spike end of the candle into the hole, and it rests securely in place. The hulking Bulgarian steps back, and the candle throws light on most of the rocky wall. Badger is impressed.

A shovel, hammer, large chisel, and hoe-like tool called a muck rake sit below the candle. Eliyah grabs the hammer.

"Badger, have you ever run a double jack?" Eliyah asks.

"I've only run a single jack," Badger says, remembering the hammer and chisel he used to bore holes that morning. "How is a double jack different?"

"A single jack is just one guy," Eliyah says as he grabs the chisel and hands it to Badger. "A double jack is two guys; that is why they call it a double jack."

"So you want me to hold the chisel, and you'll hit it with the hammer," Badger says.

Badger raises the chisel to about four feet. He secures the chisel to the wall and holds tightly. As Eliyah swings the hammer and slams it against the chisel, Badger closes his eyes and flinches.

"You must be steady, Badger," Eliyah says. "If you move the chisel, I might hit your hands."

Badger holds the chisel in place. Eliyah winds up and smacks the end of the chisel with the hammer. The chisel jumps, and a fine black powder rises from the rock. Badger turns the chisel a quarter turn after each connection, just like he did when running a single jack. Eliyah swings the hammer with powerful force, and Badger winces with every hit. Badger's arms would break like chicken bones if Eliyah missed, but Badger trusts the enormous man.

After about thirty minutes of hard hammering, the chisel sits nearly six inches into the rock. Eliyah takes a deep breath and slumps his shoulders.

"Move the chisel to the right about fifteen inches," Eliyah says.

Badger sets the chisel fifteen inches to the right and holds tightly. The young cowboy's shoulders are tight, his hands are raw, and his ears will not stop ringing.

Eliyah swings the hammer with all his considerable might. The hammer smacks the chisel, and the chisel bounces into the rock wall. Badger is tempted to close his eyes, but he remembers Eliyah's warning. Badger twists the chisel a quarter turn, and Eliyah swings the hammer again. The hammer strikes violently, and the chisel settles a little deeper into the rock wall.

"Hey, what's goin' on down there?" a man yells from inside the gatehouse.

Eliyah sets down the hammer and wipes sweat from his forehead. He sucks in a deep breath and yells, "It is cold in here. We are just hammering to keep warm."

"Nobody is gettin' any sleep with your poundin'," the man yells. "If I get you some blankets, will you stop?"

"If we were warm, we would stop," Eliyah shouts.

"I'll be back," the man yells.

"What if we're not through by then?" Badger whispers.

"If we are not through the rock in the next fifteen minutes, I am not spending all night trying. And it would be easier to sleep with some blankets."

Badger moves the chisel below the holes they have already made. Eliyah winds up and slams down the hammer. The chisel wiggles, and black powder puffs into the air. The candle lighting the tunnel has burned down nearly two inches since they started. Badger sets the chisel again, and Eliyah wallops it with the hammer. This time, the chisel doesn't jump. It sinks into the rock about two inches, like a knife jabbed into a watermelon. Badger tries to twist the chisel, but it is stuck.

"Move back, Badger," Eliyah says. "We are almost through."

The mammoth man raps the chisel three times. Each time, the chisel sinks nearly an inch. With the chisel about six inches into the rock, Eliyah slams the hammer into the rock between the three holes. The wall shudders, and dust falls from the rock. The crew leader attacks the wall fiercely again and again. After eight violent hits, a crack forms between the top two holes. With two more blows, jagged cracks form to the bottom. Eliyah swings the hammer three more times, and the triangle of rock cracks down the middle.

"Hey, stop it!" a man yells down the hole. "I got your blankets, so stop poundin' on those rocks."

"Go get the blankets," Eliyah whispers to Badger.

Badger walks slowly through the dark tunnel, leaving the candle behind. The farther he goes, the darker it is. Badger stumbles on rocks, crashing frequently to the ground. He can't see the vertical shaft that leads to the surface, but he can feel a slight breeze and hear a man fumbling with a ring of keys. Badger feels the ground with his boot toe until he locates the blankets.

"Thanks for the blankets," Badger yells up the shaft.

"Shut up and go to sleep," the man replies, assuming the prisoners are well contained.

With the blankets gathered in his arms, Badger shuffles back to Eliyah. As he approaches, he sees that Eliyah has the chisel wedged in the area they were working. The beefy builder pries out a turnip-sized rock, then an apple-sized one, then potato, and then a slurry of gooseberry-sized pebbles. Badger's stomach grumbles as he thinks about all the food-sized bits of rock Eliyah is pulling out. With two more scrapes from the chisel, Eliyah clears all the rocks from the triangular hole. Badger sees dirt on the other side.

"Isn't it usually the other way around?" Badger asks, puzzled. "Shouldn't the dirt be on top and the rocks on bottom?"

Eliyah chuckles. "Badger, you forget where we are. We dig rocks then dirt because we are digging from the inside to the outside."

It makes sense, but the backward logic spins Badger's brains a little.

"Find another chisel in that pile of tools, Badger, and help me dig," Eliyah says.

Badger scans the dark ground, but he can't see anything. The only entrance to the tunnel is through the gatehouse, and it's as dark as a cup of cowboy coffee. He squats and squints and finally notices the rounded edge of a small chisel. He grabs the chisel and begins digging out the damp dirt from the hole in the rock.

"How much farther do you think we have to dig?" Badger asks as they tear at the dirt.

"I do not know," Eliyah says. "We dig until we see moonlight—or until someone stops us."

With the pounding over, the camp above settles to sleep as Badger and Eliyah work.

Finally, Badger thrusts his chisel into the wall, and the tool plunges about six inches deep. The tired teen excitedly wiggles the chisel out of the dirt, and a ray of moonlight catches its steel like a lighthouse spotlight.

"You did it, Badger!" the crew boss says as he snorts and chortles.

Eliyah thrusts his chisel into the dirt near the hole Badger created. With three quick jabs, he widens it. Eliyah drops his digging tool and scrapes the dirt away from the gap. He then uses his hands like a dog digging after a ground squirrel to enlarge the opening. Badger breathes deeply as the cool, fresh air pours into the dark tunnel.

After five minutes of digging, the hole is about three feet wide. The builder sticks his head and arms through the hole and wiggles like a water snake. With a quick struggle, Eliyah's feet disappear through the opening.

"Come on through, Badger," Eliyah whispers. "There is a three-foot drop, so brace yourself."

Badger trusts Eliyah, but he wants a soft

landing. So he throws the blankets through the hole and then, like a giant ground squirrel, shimmies through the narrow opening. Badger stretches his arms in front of him and drops to the waiting blankets.

The cold night bites Badger's nose. The sweat on his face freezes and his ears turn bright red and burn from the chill. Badger looks up and sees the full moon glowing and the stars twinkling in the clear sky.

"It sure is cold," Badger says through chattering teeth.

"The Dutch have taken Holland," Eliyah replies.

"What's that supposed to mean?" Badger asks.

"That is what we say in Bulgaria when someone states the obvious," Eliyah explains. "You see, the Dutch are from—"

"Yeah, I get it," Badger says, handing a blanket to Eliyah.

"Clouds keep the heat in," Eliyah says. "That is why it is so cold tonight."

Badger pulls his coat tight and adjusts his scarf to ward off the cold. He pulls his cowboy hat tighter and flips his collar up to protect his ears. Badger tugs on his gloves and wiggles his fingers. His eyes cross as he watches the steam roll and tumble out of his mouth with every breath. Badger wipes his nose on the cuff of his sleeve and then wraps his blanket around his shoulders.

"Where do we go now?" Badger asks as he

eyes a twinkling star.

"We cannot stay at the camp," Eliyah says. "If they find us, they will put us in a tighter prison next time."

"But we can't stay out in the open," Badger says. "We'll freeze if we don't find shelter."

"You are right, Badger. We better warm up tonight and sneak out before first light tomorrow."

"But where can we go and not get caught?" Badger asks.

"We will sleep in the Bulgarian bunkhouse," Eliyah says without hesitation. "We Bulgarians stick together."

Chapter Three

BADGER STOPS AT A tree with cut branches, just like the one on the treasure map. He eases back into the tree, and then paces fifteen steps toward the setting sun. A hidden cavern appears to his right. Badger peers into the shallow cave and sees five canvas bags in a neat pile. Badger swallows hard. His heart races as his fingertips reach for the top bag. Badger hastily opens it and grasps at the shiny gold coins. From outside the tunnel, he hears, "Badger ... Badger ..."

"Badger, Badger! You must wake up," Eliyah hisses. "It is almost dawn."

Badger's sleepy smile becomes a frown.

"I'm awake," Badger insists, but he looks like a hibernating grizzly bear.

Eliyah rips the blanket back from the cowboy's bed, and cold air jolts Badger awake.

Badger now works like a play actor at a costume change, pulling his blue jeans and blue shirt over his faded red long underwear. He yanks on his second pair of pants and two pairs of socks. He strains to pull on his boots. Badger flops on his cowboy hat and then his tattered coat and silky scarf. Finally, he squirms his fingers into his gloves.

The bunkhouse is dark, but the windowless building is always dark. Badger hears almost fifty men snoring and thrashing around in their uncomfortable beds. Eliyah hands his companion a thin sausage rolled into a bigger circle. Badger grabs three small pickled onions out of a bowl and heads out the door. The cold air grabs at Badger's face. Steam rises from his mouth with every breath.

As the pair strides into the darkness, Badger asks, "So where are we goin'?"

"That is a question for you to answer," Eliyah says. "I have not seen anything but the worksite. You have lived here your whole life? Where is the best place to hide for a few days?"

"We're about thirty miles from my home. If we can get west of here, I know of few hidin' spots. We might even find a rancher to take us in for a day or two. But we can't hide out forever. We have to figure out who pushed Mr. Churchman into the mud pit."

"First things first, Badger," Eliyah says. "We cannot do anything if we are in a jail cell."

"The sheriff will be comin' in from Rogerson to the east," Badger says.

"Then let us head west," Eliyah says, turning

and loping into the darkness.

Badger and Eliyah approach the deep canyon tentatively. In years past, a trail ran down into the bottom of the canyon. After a quick wade across the narrow Salmon Falls Creek, the trail was easy to reach on the other side. But that is all underwater now. During the past two years of the dam's construction, water has filled in behind the dam. A perilous suspension bridge has replaced the easy crossing. Boards tied to rope form a platform just wide enough for a wagon to pass, and the upper two ropes provide a crude railing and some added support.

I'm scared to cross this thing in the daytime, Badger thinks. I must be crazy to cross it in the dark.

Badger grabs one of the rope railings and steps onto the first board like someone walking in tall grass next to a rattlesnake den. He is careful to place his foot in the center of each board. As Eliyah steps onto the bridge, the planks sway. Badger grabs a rope railing with both hands. The terrified teen has watched wagons with two horses cross this bridge, so he knows it will hold up their weight. But knowing that does little to ease the fear welling up inside him.

The two fugitives slink across the creaky bridge. They measure each step and strain to see each board. With a sheriff soon to be chasing them, Badger wants to run, but he forces himself to be careful as the bridge sways beneath them. Badger holds his breath as he steps from the last board onto the canyon's western edge with Eliyah quick on his heels.

"We have a lot of good reasons to get out of here," Eliyah says, striding away. "Let us go."

THE SUN CLIMBS SLOWLY above Badger's left shoulder. Badger is grateful for the light but disappointed with how little warmth it provides. They are about a mile west of the dam now. They have just crested a small hill that opens up to a wide, sagebrush-covered plain. With the hill in the way, the two refugees no longer see the canyon. Badger is nearly jogging to keep up with the long-striding Eliyah. Suddenly, the giant of a man stops.

"Shhh, shhh," Eliyah says as he closes his eyes to focus on listening. "Do you hear that?"

Am I walkin' like a buffalo? Badger wonders. *I didn't think I was that loud.* Badger bows his head slightly and tilts his left ear toward the hilly plain in front of him. Badger hears something too.

"Is that a wagon," Badger asks, "or a posse?"

"Wagon," Eliyah says.

"We should hide in that tall brush until it passes," Eliyah says, pointing to a patch of sagebrush about ten yards off the road.

Badger worries the sagebrush won't provide enough cover for the massive Bulgarian, but he sees nowhere else to hide. *I've seen a thousand-pound steer hide in a patch of sagebrush,* Badger thinks. *And Eliyah is only half that size—or I guess*

34

a quarter, or would it be a third? I hate fractions. Anyway, we should be well hidden.

The two reach it and crouch behind its twisted branches, carefully peeking out as the wagon approaches. A couple horses pull the wagon, a simple, uncovered buckboard. Percy Reed, Badger's best friend, sits in the middle of its seat. If Badger looks like a badger, then Percy looks a little bit like a weasel. He is neat and tidy, but he wears the dust of the trail.

Percy holds the reins snugly, his attention focused on the road. When the young driver is about to pass them, Badger jumps from his hidden nest like a cat pouncing on a mouse. Percy shrieks and snaps his whip in Badger's direction. Badger jumps back and rolls into a heap.

"Get back, thief!" Percy yells as he flicks the whip again.

"Percy, it's me," Badger says as he raises his hands in the air.

Percy squints his beady eyes as he takes in the familiar voice. "What are you doin' out here, Badger?"

"I hired on with the canal company to help build the dam," Badger says.

"Well, that explains why you're thirty miles from your mom's place at Rye Flat, but why aren't you at the work camp?"

"We got into a little trouble," Badger admits sheepishly.

"Why am I not surprised?" Percy says as he tilts his neat new cowboy hat and straightens his gray vest. "You should stick to herdin' cows."

"I tried to hire on with several ranches, but they don't have much work in the winter. And

I didn't wanna be like every other cow-punchin' drifter, just sweepin' dirt outta pool halls or—"

"And now you're in trouble again," Percy interrupts.

"We could use your help." Badger pulls his hat off his head and bows for mercy before Percy.

"Every time I help you, I end up riskin' my life," Percy says.

"It won't be like that at all. We just need somewhere to hide for a day or two."

"We?" Percy asks. "Why do you keep sayin' 'we'?"

Badger glances back at the sagebrush but can't see his older friend anywhere.

"I'm here with a Bulgarian worker named Eliyah," Badger explains. "He was accused of pushin' the foreman into the concrete, but he says he didn't do it."

"Mr. Churchman?" Percy asks. "I know him, and there are probably two hundred people who could have pushed him into the concrete—and another two hundred who wouldn't say anythin' if they saw it."

"How do you know Mr. Churchman?" Badger asks.

"Well, I got tired of peddlin' vegetables back home, so I got the contract to supply beef to the work camp. I bought a dozen steers and am leasin' some grass over on Whiskey Slough. Once a week, I bring butchered beef to the camp. The pay is better than sellin' watermelons."

"Why don't you just work at your dad's

store back in Three Creek?" Badger asks.

"I tried for a little while, but the pay isn't great."

"He doesn't pay you what you're worth?"

"He doesn't pay me at all."

Badger chuckles.

Eliyah rises from the patch of sagebrush. Percy recoils with a gasp.

"Percy, this is Eliyah," Badger says.

"It's nice to meet you," Percy says, his eyes round.

Eliyah nods at Percy.

"Will you help us?" Badger asks.

"Wait here. I'll make my delivery and ask around at the cook shack. The cook seems to know everythin' that goes on in the camp."

"Badger," Eliyah says, "you could go back and help Percy look for clues."

"But Nikos might kill me!" Badger says.

"I heard what he said, cowboy," Eliyah says as he removes his derby hat and unwraps the gray knit scarf all the Bulgarians wear. "He told you to be quiet. In Bulgaria, we say, 'A closed mouth catches no flies.' Keep your mouth closed and look around quietly. You should be fine. Wear my hat and scarf. If anybody asks, say you are Serbian. Two other Serbians work with us Bulgarians."

Eliyah removes Badger's cowboy hat, and Badger pulls off his scarf. Badger places Eliyah's hat on his head. A small hat on Eliyah is a large hat on Badger, and the derby hat falls down to the teen's eyebrows. The big man's knit scarf is almost as tall as Badger. Eliyah wraps the scarf around Badger's neck and then his mouth and ears until only Badger's eyes are exposed. Eliyah steps back and looks at Badger.

"You look cold," Eliyah says, chuckling. "But you do not look like Badger. Call yourself Marko, and nobody will know."

"Let's go, Badg—I mean, Marko. They're expectin' my delivery," Percy says as he points to the meat in his wagon.

"Be careful, boys," Eliyah say. "The sheriff will arrest you if he finds you. Remember, many are born human, but some die donkeys. Nikos is a donkey and just might throw you in the dam if you make too much noise."

Badger grins as he pictures Nikos with long floppy ears and a buck-toothed mule face. "We'll meet you here in a couple hours," Badger says through his smile.

Percy shakes the reins, and the wagon rolls down the road toward the worksite.

PERCY AND BADGER SEE people scurrying around the site, but very few men are working. One group is rallying around an angry man. He shouts and gestures, and the onlookers respond angrily in unison. Another group looks like its members are packing to leave.

Percy rolls up to the meal hall and stops the wagon with a jerk.

"I'm gonna lie low," Badger says. "I think I'll warm up at the Bulgarian bunkhouse."

Percy jumps off the wagon and strides into the mess hall.

"The beef is here," Percy says.

Two men in aprons promptly scurry out to retrieve the meat. Percy saunters up to the cook shack's counter, where a petite, middle-aged woman stoops over a pot of stew, stirring it like a witch creating a magic potion.

The woman looks up from her work and says, "Hello, Percy. I do not have payment for you today. You will have to talk to the engineer, Rolf Schmitz."

"Why's that, Fanni?" Percy asks as he picks through a bowl of pickles. "Mr. Churchman usually has my payment ready."

Percy leans on the high counter. He tips his hat to the side, grins from one side of his mouth, and nods his head. Fanni guffaws and rolls her eyes. Percy is trying to play it cool, but Fanni just thinks he is odd.

"Well, there was an accident at the worksite yesterday, and Mr. Churchman fell into the concrete," Fanni says as she tugs on her dark blue dress and straightens her grease-spattered apron.

"Wow!" Percy says, faking surprise. "How'd that happen?"

"I am not sure," Fanni says. "Word around camp is that the big Bulgarian and some new kid pushed him in. But, really, it could have been anyone."

"Is that why there's so much activity in the camp?" Percy asks. "The whole camp is busy, but no one is workin'."

"That big Bulgarian was the only one of them who could speak English," Fanni says as she tosses a pinch of salt in the stew. "With him gone, the whole crew of fifty Bulgarians is leaving."

"What about the rest of the camp?" Percy asks around a mouthful of pickles as the two aproned men lug in the last of the beef.

"I think they are forming some kind of mob," Fanni says. She adjusts the bun on the top of her head. "I think they want to find the big Bulgarian and the new kid."

Percy gulps as his worry for Badger fizzes up like a shook-up bottle of soda water. He forces a grin for Fanni and looks at the door.

"Well, I better go over to the engineer's office to check on my payment," Percy says.

He turns on his heel and marches for the door.

BADGER SNEAKS INTO THE Bulgarian bunkhouse. All of the Bulgarians are packing. They place their changes of clothes and other small belongings into a blanket and tie the four corners together to form a bag. They all stop and look suspiciously at Badger. They recognize Eliyah's hat and scarf.

"Dobro utro," Stephano says to Badger in Bulgarian. "Dali Eliyah nared?"

"Uh, I don't speak Bulgarian," Badger replies.

"Dobro utro," Stephano says. "Good

morning." Stephano has an accent just like Eliyah's, but his voice isn't as deep. Badger smiles at how Stephano says *good* like Badger says *food*.

"Dobro utro," Badger replies.

"Eliyah?" Stephano ask.

"Yeah, Eliyah is fine. He's waitin' for me just west of here."

Stephano scrunches his eyebrows, shakes his head, and shrugs.

"Sorry," Badger says. "Eliyah," and Badger points to the west and smiles. Stephano nods and returns the smile.

Without Eliyah, these guys can talk only among themselves, Badger thinks. *They really can't work here without him.*

"Nikos subira tulpa," Stephano says.

Badger shakes his head and shrugs.

"Nikos," Stephano says as he points to the angry mob. Stephano puts his hand around his own neck.

"Nikos is chokin'," Badger guesses, but he immediately knows he is wrong. "Nikos has a sore throat. No, that's not right either. Nikos is gatherin' a lynch mob to come after Eliyah!"

Stephano shakes his head yes. Badger shakes his head no. His stomach spins and his face turns green.

"We have to do somethin'," Badger says.

Stephano shrugs his lack of understanding.

"Nikos," Badger says. "Stop. Stop Nikos!"

Stephano nods vigorously. The two step toward the door and out into the frigid January air.

PERCY PEEKS HIS HEAD into the engineer's office. The well-kempt building is small and well lit. A man with glasses sits at the desk and runs his fingers through his thinning hair. Blueprints and scratch paper cover the desk, and designs and sketches adorn the walls. Mr. Schmitz looks up at Percy.

"Hello there," Mr. Schmitz says. He tilts his head down to look at Percy above the glasses on his nose. "What can I help you with?"

"Well, sir, I was told Mr. Churchman is unavailable, and I need payment for the beef I just brought."

Mr. Schmitz sits up and straightens his gray vest. He brushes back a few stray gray hairs. Mr. Schmitz has black bushy eyebrows that curl up like a smile. His smiling eyebrows contrast with his sour face. He looks like he walked into a just-used outhouse. Mr. Schmitz wiggles his nose and takes a deep breath before responding. "Win Churchman was killed yesterday, and things around here are a little disorganized. I am losing a quarter of the crew, so we will only need half the regular amount of beef next week."

"Um, I can't kill half a steer," Percy says with a snicker. "I could skip next week's delivery and bring another beef in two weeks."

"Yes, yes, that would work," Mr. Schmitz says. "I cannot pay you today. Win Churchman handled the moneybox and books. In fact, he managed most everything around here, so not much is getting done. The company is sending a bookkeeper here tomorrow to handle payroll. Could you come back then for your payment?"

"Sure," Percy says with a sigh. He tilts his head down and stares up at Mr. Schmitz so he will know Percy is annoyed. "I'll be back about the same time tomorrow."

Percy nods goodbye and heads outside. A few Bulgarians are leaving the camp carrying small bundles. Percy jumps into his wagon to wait for Badger.

Where is Badger, Percy wonders, *and why do I let him drag me into his troubles?* Percy looks to the heavens for an answer.

BADGER AND STEPHANO WANDER over to the angry mob. Nikos is surrounded by almost forty Greeks and about twice that number of other Europeans, workers who came from Italy, Spain, Austria, Sweden, Montenegro, Poland, France, and Ireland. With the foreman gone, they are all out of work and bored. Nikos yells furiously, and the mob shouts its reply in unison.

Badger scans the crowd nervously. *Keep your mouth shut—or you might be the next one over the edge,* Badger remembers hearing Nikos say. *But I gotta do somethin'.* The disguised cowboy walks to the front of the mob. Badger stands silently a few feet from Stephano as the crowd's rage builds.

"We cannot let Eliyah get away with murder!" Nikos yells.

"No!" the mob responds.

"We have to hunt him down!" Nikos yells.

"He must face justice!"

"Yes!" the mob replies. "Justice!"

"Someone grab a rope!" Nikos shouts. "We will hunt him down and hang him!"

"Hang him!" the mob agrees.

"That is not justice," Badger blurts loud enough for everyone to hear. The whole mob shifts angry gazes to Badger. The teen pulls on his scarf to make sure it is still covering his face. Remembering he is supposed to be Marko the Serbian, Badger deepens his voice and makes it a little raspy. "If you hang him without a trial, it is not justice. It is murder."

"Eliyah is guilty!" Nikos yells. "We all know that, and justice demands he be hanged."

Badger swallows his fear and speaks in his bad Serbian accent, "Justice is a sheriff, judge, and jury. He deserves a chance to defend himself in a court of law."

"He deserves a short rope and a long drop!" Nikos yells. The mob does not respond. The individuals in the mob murmur to one another and many turn toward their warm bunkhouses.

"If you kill like this," Badger rasps, "you could be charged with murder."

A few people leave the scene.

"Who are you?" Nikos asks. He no longer yells, but his eyes stab into Badger like a wolf glaring at a mountain lion.

"I am Marko the Serbian," Badger says, but it sounds more like a question.

Nikos stalks closer to Badger, glaring. With

Nikos's attention elsewhere, everyone except a few Greeks and Stephano leave.

"So, Marko, why have I not seen you around camp?" Nikos asks.

"I am new," Badger says, his accent wavering.

"You remind me of a cowboy who found trouble here." Nikos moves around Badger like a crow circling a carcass.

"I do not know how to ride a horse," Badger says.

"Marko, da vurvim," Stephano says, nodding toward the Bulgarian bunkhouse.

Badger doesn't know what Stephano said, but he nods in agreement. Badger and Stephano step away without turning their backs to Nikos. When they are a safe distance, they spin around and retreat.

"Keep walking, cowboy!" Nikos yells. "And when you see Eliyah, tell him he is next! I will get rid of anyone I need to—including you, cowboy!"

A chill runs along Badger's spine. *If Eliyah is next,* Badger wonders, *then who was first—Mr. Churchman or Marko the Serbian?*

Chapter Four

BADGER AND PERCY ROLL steadily along. The
wagon creaks and groans, and the two teens sway
from side to side with every bump. Without the
heavy load, the wagon bounces over every rock. Its
seat is wide enough for two people, and the back
of the wagon is about four feet wide and eight feet
long. The wheel spokes spin wildly as Percy's two
horses pull the light load. As they approach the
spot where they left Eliyah, the Bulgarian climbs
out from behind a sagebrush and approaches the
road. The wagon rolls to Eliyah, and Percy pulls the
horses to a stop.

"What did you find out?" Eliyah asks as dust
covers the meeting.

"It doesn't look good, Eliyah," Badger says,
returning the big man's hat and scarf. "Seems like
anybody could've done it, but everyone thinks you

did it."

"That's not what I heard, Badger," Percy says. "Fanni thinks both of you were in on it."

Badger grimaces. "It doesn't look good for either of us. I went to the bunkhouse, and the Bulgarians are packin' up and leavin'."

"Why?" Eliyah asks.

"Because you're gone," Badger says. "You're the only one who speaks both languages."

"I need to go back then," Eliyah says. "My people need these jobs."

"I wouldn't do that either," Badger says. "A mob was gatherin' to lynch you—"

"Both of you," Percy interrupts.

"Yeah, both of us." Badger is a little annoyed that Percy reminds him of how deeply he is involved in this crime.

"Why is a mob gathering?" Eliyah asks. "I thought everybody hated Mr. Churchman."

"They did," Badger says, "but everybody is outta work for now—and mad. Nikos really had them fired up against you. And when I stepped in to defend you, Nikos threatened me too."

"We need to lie low for a couple of days until everything calms down," Eliyah says.

"Could we stay with you, Percy?" Badger asks.

"That's not a bad idea," Percy replies. "I usually get paid today and then use the money to hire a couple cowhands to help me move my steers. You guys could help me instead."

Badger looks like a thief who has had his

plunder stolen. *I need a place to hide,* Badger thinks, *not a back-breaking job without pay.*

"We would be happy to help you," Eliyah says. "In Bulgaria, we say, 'A lazy man works like a bug, eats like a bear.' I do not want to be a bug or a bear."

"Yeah, yeah, we'll help you," Badger mutters.

As Eliyah climbs up beside Percy, Badger swings into the back, settles onto the boards, and hangs onto the side. Percy shakes the reins and the wagon rolls toward Whiskey Slough.

PERCY'S SMALL RANCH AT Whiskey Slough is falling apart. In fact, it can hardly be called a ranch. Smoke trickles out a crooked chimney at the top of a single-room cabin, which is really just a shack. A small log barn, barely big enough for three horses, stands about twenty steps from the cabin. Its roof looks like a leaky rain barrel, and the paddock is a three-pole fence that is broken in two places. A sorry-looking apple tree clings to life next to a frozen stream. Behind the barn are blood and other steer parts from Percy's morning activities.

Badger had hoped to warm up in Percy's meager cabin, but most of the heat from the stove scurries up the chimney. Badger focuses all his energy on not shivering. He wiggles his toes. He rubs his cheeks. *I swear I can feel ice crystals formin' in my body,* Badger thinks as the cold grips him from the inside out.

Percy has three horses saddled and ready to

ride. Short bursts of steam blow out their nostrils as they wait. The horses fidget and switch their tails up and down.

"You ready to go?" Percy asks as he unties his horse. "You should be, since I saddled the horses while you were warmin' up."

Percy is riding his dependable white horse, Snowball. A black horse named Midnight awaits Badger, and a sorrel horse named Socks is ready for Eliyah.

"Let's get this done and find somewhere warm," Badger says, pulling Midnight away from the fence.

"I do not know how to be a cowboy," Eliyah says with an uncomfortable grin. "But I learn fast."

"First thing you need to do is tighten your cinch," Badger says.

"Do what?" Eliyah asks.

"The cinch, the cinch—that leather strap that holds your saddle on the horse's back."

Eliyah pulls on the strap, and Socks slumps and sways.

"Not too tight," Badger says. "You should be able to fit a couple fingers under the cinch."

Eliyah loosens the cinch, and the horse relaxes like a man at a community potluck who unbuttons the top button on his pants. Badger steps beside Eliyah and grabs the end of the cinch.

"I can't tell you how to tie it off; I'll just show you," Badger says.

Badger pulls the cinch down through the D-ring, pulls the leather across the cinch, back up through the D-ring, and back down under the loose leather. He pulls it tight, and the cinch pulls against itself in a secure fastening.

"You're all ready to go," Badger says. "Just swing on."

"Swing how?" Eliyah says.

"Put your foot in the stirrup, and climb into the saddle."

Eliyah puts his right foot in the left stirrup.

"Wait, wait, wait. You need to put your other foot in the stirrup," Badger says, trying not to be annoyed. "Let me show you."

Badger puts his left foot in the stirrup. He bounces twice, and in one graceful motion lifts his body up and swings his right leg over the saddle until his backside slides into it. Badger isn't an expert cowboy, but he looks like he belongs.

"Just like that," Badger says.

"We need to get goin' before it gets dark," Percy says, swinging onto his horse.

Eliyah puts his foot in the stirrup and pulls his leg straight. But instead of rising into the saddle, the saddle rolls to the side until the stirrup is nearly to the ground. Eliyah's horse steps to the right and Eliyah stumbles out of the stirrup. Percy laughs out loud. Badger laughs quietly to himself.

"Is my cinch too loose?" Eliyah asks.

"Your cinch is plenty tight," Badger explains. "I've never seen anybody as big as you climb on a horse."

Eliyah pushes the saddle horn, and the saddle rotates back into position. He tries to swing on, but the saddle slips again.

"Maybe you could lead him up next to a fence and climb on from the fence," Badger says.

Eliyah leads Socks next to a fence. He starts to climb the fence, but the wooden pole breaks under his weight. Percy laughs again. Badger holds back a laugh, making him snort like a pig. Percy laughs harder. Socks waits patiently as he watches the giant make a mess of Percy's corral. But Badger is certain Socks rolled his eyes.

Eliyah pulls his horse forward and tries another pole. He lifts his massive frame up about three feet and grabs the saddle horn. He hesitates a moment and then awkwardly swings his leg over the saddle. His backside thuds into the seat. Eliyah wiggles, searching for a comfortable spot. He doesn't find one.

Socks, who has a big white stripe on his forehead and white front legs up to his knees, tucks in his tail as his hind legs shake with stress. The horse spreads his front legs out and locks his knees.

"Okay, I am on," Eliyah says. He looks as happy as a little kid riding an elephant at the circus. Socks looks as troubled as a dog being ridden by a little kid. "How do I make him go?"

"Kick him to make him go," Badger says. "Pull back on the reins to make him stop. Pull left to make him go left, and pull right to make him go right."

"Will I hurt him if I kick him?"

"Don't kick him like you're angry; just tap him with your heels," Badger says.

Eliyah touches his heels to Socks. Socks' legs wobble like a baby fawn taking its first steps. Eliyah kicks a little bit harder, and Socks picks up one foot but quickly puts it down again. Eliyah kicks Socks twice more. With legs shaking, Socks lies down.

"I think you're too heavy for Socks," Badger says.

"He's the biggest horse I have," Percy says. "Me and Badger can get the steers moved. Do you mind a little blood? if not, could you clean up the mess behind the barn?"

"I do not mind blood," Eliyah says, "and I want to earn my room and board."

"Just put all the guts inside the hide and fold it up," Percy says. "And throw some dirt on the blood, so the coyotes don't come in to lick it up. Everything can go in the barn for now."

Eliyah swings off Socks, and the horse takes a deep breath and relaxes. Socks isn't injured, but he is sweating and looks like he just ran a race without even leaving the yard.

In a cloud of dust and steam, Badger and Percy ride to a nearby pasture. Accustomed to the routine, the steers are waiting near the gate. Percy opens the gate, and Badger jogs his horse around the herd.

Badger relaxes as he rides and thinks about their dilemma. *It's obvious Nikos pushed in Mr. Churchman. So how did he do it ... and why?*

After more than an hour of Badger's gentle prompting, the last fat steer saunters slowly through the gate. The beasts seem to smile as they drop their heads into the fresh feed.

"Thanks for your help," Percy says.

"I probably owe you one," Badger replies.

"One!" Percy raises his voice. "You owe me one? I think you owe me three or maybe four."

54

"That's not right," Badger says. "I made up for that ride to Mr. Gaar's place. I showed you how to waltz so you could dance with Bertha Jo Stillwell."

"Yeah, I remember," Percy says, giving Badger the stink eye as he closes the gate behind the last steer. "And what you showed me sure wasn't dancin'. I stepped on her foot every other step. She laughed at me and said I was dancin' the one-step— the one-step, Badger!"

"It's not my fault she doesn't have any rhythm," Badger says as Percy remounts. "Look, I appreciate your help, and I'll make it up to you."

"You'll try," Percy says, forcing a grin as the two ride back toward the little ranch to warm up. "And I will always bail you out."

Percy's right, Badger thinks. *I'm not just gonna talk about makin' it right. I'm really gonna make it up to Percy this time.*

THE NEXT MORNING, BADGER wakes up cold. Percy is already up stoking the fire in the rounded-log cabin. Lying in bed, Badger can see his breath as if he were outside. Badger pulls his blanket closer, trying vainly to start the day warm. Badger's toes ache; his feet haven't been truly warm in weeks. Badger needs to pee but remembers the outhouse is thirty paces around the back of the cabin. As cold as it is, he decides to hold it.

"Mornin', Badger. I've got to go back to the dam to get my pay," Percy says as he mixes a mysterious white glob in a bowl. "After breakfast, could you help me hook up the team and then chop some firewood?"

"Sure," Badger says, looking around. The sleepy cowboy notices a table with some books and a ledger and a couple shelves holding cups, plates, and cooking tools. He sees bunk beds, the top bed with an unkempt blanket and the bottom one with a neatly folded blanket.

"Where's Eliyah?" Badger asks.

"He's outside drawin' water from the spring," Percy says.

Badger yawns and slithers out of his blanket. He starts a stretch but stops abruptly as a chill climbs up his spine. Badger scooches up to the warm stove, pretending to want to help Percy with breakfast. Greasy smoke fills the cabin as lard pops and boils in the pan. His best friend is frying either pancakes or biscuits; Badger isn't sure which. They're too thick to be pancakes but too thin to be biscuits. *Pancakes are always delicious,* Badger thinks as he chokes on the smoke. *These look more like biscuits.* Badger doesn't really care, because he is hungry enough to eat either.

A bundled-up Eliyah steps inside and sets a bucket of water next to the front door. He unwinds his scarf and pulls off his coat.

"Good morning, Badger," Eliyah says.

"Mornin'," Badger says, intentionally leaving out the *good.*

"The sun is shining, Badger," Eliyah says with a genuine smile, "and I am as fresh as a pickle. It really is a good morning."

Badger rolls his eyes. He's pretty sure Eliyah sleeps with a smile on his face.

Percy lays out three plates, no two alike. He scoops a pastry onto each plate and returns the pan to the stove.

Badger's biscuit is blackened on top and doughy on bottom. The hungry teen tries to stab his fork into the blackened side, but the biscuit resists his efforts. It is as solid as a cast-iron stove.

Badger flips the biscuit over and peels the doughy side away from the burned side. He tosses a bit of the doughy biscuit into his mouth and chews. Its flavor dances over Badger's tongue, and he freezes. *Yuck!* Badger thinks. *I'm gonna have to lick a skunk's tail to get this taste outta my mouth.*

Badger closes his eyes and struggles not to gag. He swallows the lump of dough, and a rusty-chimney aftertaste licks up his throat.

Incredibly hungry, Badger braves another two bites and swallows down a big gulp of coffee, floating black flakes and all. The bitter coffee tastes almost as bad as the biscuit.

Percy, seeing that Badger has finished the edible part of his biscuit, asks, "You ready for another?"

"No, thanks. I'm full," Badger lies.

"Be sure to put a couple in your pocket for lunch," Percy says. "They're just as good then as they are now."

"I'm sure they are," Badger says, grabbing a couple and hoping they will get a little better sitting in his pocket.

"I better get movin'," Percy says. "I wanna be there when the bookkeeper shows up—just in case the camp runs outta money. The way things are goin' there, I don't trust I'll get paid at all."

"I'll help you hitch up," Badger says as he rubs his unsettled belly. "Hey, Percy, could you ask around a bit more about Mr. Churchman?"

"Sure," Percy says as the two teens put on their coats, scarves, gloves, and hats. "Want me to ask anyone particular?"

"Nothin' happens at the worksite without Fanni knowin' about it," Badger says.

"I talked with her yesterday," Percy says as the two head out into the cold.

"Talk with her again," Badger says. "She has had three meals to hear the gossip. And I'm worried about Nikos possibly comin' after us."

"I'll see what I can find, but my first job is to get paid."

"Please find somethin'. It's too cold to live on the run."

"I'll try, Badger. I'll try."

Chapter Five

THE WORKSITE IS AS tense as a classroom on report-card day. All the Bulgarians have left. Nikos is again whipping up an angry mob, but no voice of reason calms the onlookers today. Percy parks in front of the cook shack and scurries inside.

Percy's timing is perfect. Fanni is cleaning up from breakfast and has leftover bacon and pancakes. Percy grabs a plate and fills it with crisp strips of pork and perfectly fluffy pancakes. He smothers them with butter and maple syrup. Percy eats like this will be his last good meal for a week—and it will be. As he eats, he interrogates Fanni.

"So have you found out what happened to Mr. Churchman?" Percy asks.

"I told you yesterday," Fanni says. "That Bulgarian and new kid did it."

Percy cringes. He tries to distract from his

reaction by asking, "What's the latest gossip?"

"Well, Percy, I do not like to gossip," Fanni says with a wag of her finger. "But I did hear that Rolf Schmitz owed Mr. Churchman a gambling debt. I guess his debt went away, though, since Mr. Churchman is not here to collect it."

"That's interestin'," Percy says between bites. "Do you think Mr. Schmitz pushed Mr. Churchman into the concrete?"

"I do not know. But a coyote will not attack unless it gets cornered," Fanni says.

"Do you think Mr. Schmitz is a coyote?" Percy asks.

"I do not think so, but maybe. I do know that a new man who ate here last Friday might be a coyote," Fanni says in not quite a whisper, her eyes shining as she delights in sharing her gossip. "He was here to sell Mr. Churchman a life-insurance policy."

"A life-insurance policy," Percy repeats. "I wonder what that's about."

"Makes me wonder too," Fanni says as she lifts stacks of thirty clean tin plates at a time and puts them on a shelf on the back wall.

"With a life-insurance policy, someone gets paid if the person dies, right?" Percy asks.

"I think that is right," Fanni replies.

"But no one found a body," Percy says.

"I think it is obvious he went in. The, how do you say, depression was deep enough, and his hat was on top," Fanni says, wiping the counter between the kitchen and dining areas. "A few months ago, a mountain lion jumped into the concrete, and men searched for two days without finding the carcass. They must have liked the lion better than Mr. Churchman. They only searched for him for thirty minutes."

Percy chuckles. He wouldn't have searched long for Mr. Churchman either.

"I think enough people witnessed it for an insurance payout," Fanni continues.

"I wonder who gets the money," Percy says, trying to be casual.

"Why do you want to know?" Fanni says.

Percy's eyes widen and his heart races. He can't give Eliyah and Badger away, or the entire camp will know where they are by dinnertime.

"I'm just catchin' up on the latest gossip," Percy says with a shrug. "I don't really have anybody to talk to out at my place."

"What about the cowboys you hire to help you? Are they not still around?" Fanni asks.

Percy tries not to squirm. "They're not big talkers. My Aunt Maude taught me to gossip back home at the store, and the cowboys don't live up to her chatty standards."

Percy grins like an egg-sucking dog with feathers on his cheeks. He hopes Fanni's buying what he's selling. He hurriedly shoves the rest of his second breakfast into his mouth.

His cheeks stuffed, Percy says, "I better get over to Mr. Schmitz's office. I really need to get paid."

"Be careful out there," Fanni says. "Nikos

has the men pretty angry about being out of work until a new foreman is hired. I am afraid of what they might do."

Percy stands up straight to make his too-big bite slide down the chute. He winces as he swallows hard. "Whattaya think they'll do?" Percy asks.

"I do not know, but I worry about anyone they decide to go after," Fanni says.

Percy grimaces and heads for the door

"See you next week," Fanni says, giving Percy a slight wave.

"Oh, I won't be back next week," Percy says.

"I'm not sure any of us will be here next week," Fanni says with a sigh.

PERCY PEEKS HIS HEAD inside the engineer's office. Sitting behind the desk, Mr. Schmitz looks haggard, like he has been doing the work of two men.

"Good mornin'," Percy calls through the open doorway. "I was told to come back today to get my money for the beef I delivered yesterday."

"Of course," Mr. Schmitz says. "The bookkeeper has reviewed your claim, and I have your payment here."

Mr. Schmitz starts counting out Percy's payment as the teen takes a seat across from the engineer.

"I hear you run a poker game here at the worksite," Percy says.

"Well, I play poker, but Win Churchman was

the one who put the games together," Mr. Schmitz says.

"I bet he was a pretty good player and lots of people owed him money," Percy says.

Mr. Schmitz looks at Percy. The young rancher squirms in his chair and looks at his hands to avoid making eye contact with Mr. Schmitz. *I'm pretty sure Mr. Schmitz is on to me,* Percy thinks.

"Win Churchman liked to play, but he was not a very good player," Mr. Schmitz finally replies.

"So who owed him money?" Percy asks.

"Win owed money to everyone he played with," Mr. Schmitz says. "Based on our poker games, Win Churchman is the only one who benefits from Win Churchman being dead."

Percy scrapes the pile of coins into his hand, stands, and drops the payment into his pocket.

"A rumor is going around camp that you were seen with the kid, Badger. I am guessing you at least know where he is and probably Eliyah too," Mr. Schmitz says slowly and clearly as Percy grins like a tail-wagging dog and inches toward the door. "The sheriff has been wired and should eventually get out here, but he seems to be taking his time. They need to go to Twin Falls and turn themselves in, and I say this because I like Eliyah. It is no secret Nikos hates the Bulgarian crew leader, and he is gathering a lynch mob outside. If they find Eliyah and the kid, they will not hold back."

"If I see them, I'll let them know," Percy says, emphasizing if to give the appearance that he doesn't know where they are. "But how can they get

to Twin Falls if crossin' the bridge by the dam is the only way to get there?"

"The water is frozen a mile or two upstream, and they could cross there," Mr. Schmitz says. "If they hurry, they could catch up with the mule train heading back to Rogerson. They might even bump into the sheriff on one of the trains. I wired him two days ago, and he should eventually be coming out."

Percy nods and scurries out the door like a mouse with cheese in his cheeks. Nikos still stands before the mob, but now he has a rope in his raised fist. Percy flees to his wagon.

PERCY'S HORSES ARE SWEATING and breathing heavily when his wagon rolls up to the ranch. Eliyah and Badger are stacking the wood they spent the past two hours chopping. Badger wipes sweat from his brow and rubs his sore hands.

Percy pulls the horses to a stop and applies the brake to his wagon. He jumps down and runs to Badger and Eliyah like Paul Revere riding through Boston.

"You two need to turn yourselves in," Percy says through gasps.

"Whattaya mean, Percy?" Badger asks. "We can't find out who killed Mr. Churchman if we're in jail."

"Nikos and his mob of vigilantes are comin' after you," Percy says. "They are all riled up and want to hang you both."

"We should get out of here, Badger," Eliyah says. "We can at least tell our side of the story to a jury, but this mob already believes we are guilty."

Badger nods. "Did you find out anythin' else, Percy?"

"Fanni the cook said Mr. Schmitz and Mr. Churchman had a high-stakes card game," Percy says. "She said Mr. Schmitz owed Mr. Churchman a lot of money. But when I asked Mr. Schmitz about it, he said Mr. Churchman owed everybody in the game money."

"That doesn't make much sense," Badger says as he and Eliyah put on their coats. "Is that all you heard?"

"Well, Fanni also mentioned that a life-insurance salesman visited Mr. Churchman last week," Percy says.

"So somebody's probably gonna get paid a lot of money," Badger says.

"And if you can find out who, then you'll probably find the killer," Percy says.

"What about Nikos?" Badger asks as he wraps his scarf around his neck and puts on his hat.

"I suppose he could've done it to frame Eliyah," Percy says.

"Well, that makes the most sense to me," Badger says.

"Well, make sense of this," Percy says as he points in the direction of the dam worksite. "An angry mob is lookin' to kill—"

"You are right," Eliyah says. "We need to leave now, Badger."

"Follow the creek for a half mile," Percy says, pointing to the small stream flowing through his ranch. "If you walk in the creek bed, the water will cover your tracks. Head straight east when the

creek turns north. The water should be frozen up there, and you should be able to get to Rogerson without bein' seen. I saw an empty mule train makin' ready to head back to Rogerson. Maybe you could hitch a ride."

"Can we borrow your horses?" Badger asks.

"My horses can't carry Eliyah," Percy says, "and I just left the worksite with two horses. If the mob shows up here and I don't have two horses, it'll look awful suspicious."

"Besides, a horse is heavier and would leave deeper footprints in the creek," Eliyah says. "The mob will not be able to track us on foot."

"But our feet will get wet," Badger complains.

"Whenever your feet start hurtin' just think about a rope around your neck," Percy says. "That should help ease the pain."

"That's not funny, Percy," Badger says.

"I'm not tryin' to be funny," Percy replies. "I'm tryin' to get you movin'."

"Percy is right," Eliyah says as he steps into the icy water. "We must go."

The two hunted workers splash along the creek bed. The stream is shallow and more like walking through a puddle than a creek. They turn east and hike with Eliyah in the lead and Badger closer than his shadow.

Percy waves goodbye to his friends and then looks around his yard for any evidence the two were there. He unhitches his horses and leads them to the creek where Badger and Eliyah stepped. His horses take big drinks and then plod along the stream's bank. Just as Percy hopes, his horses' hoof prints cover up Badger's and Eliyah's footprints.

Chapter Six

BADGER GINGERLY STEPS ONTO the ice. As cold as it has been, Badger is pretty sure the ice will hold him. But he still worries. *I would hate for my whole body to get as wet as my feet,* Badger thinks. The water below the ice is nearly freezing, and the winter air would turn deadly if Badger and Eliyah were wholly wet.

Eliyah steps confidently onto the ice and moves with quick, measured steps. The ice whines and groans, but it doesn't crack under the weight of the mammoth man. The iced-over reservoir is about fifty feet across, and Eliyah strides halfway in about six long steps.

Badger looks like a four-legged animal crossing the ice. Each of his steps is cautious, and he keeps his feet wide apart. Despite being careful, Badger's feet slip out from under him and he falls hard on his back, knocking the air from his lungs. Badger strains to breathe and finally relaxes enough to fill his lungs. He climbs to his knees. As he tries to rise to his feet, his boots slide and he falls back down like a dropped marionette. Badger lies motionless on the ice, waiting for a puppeteer to pull his strings.

"You need better boots, cowboy," Eliyah says with a laugh, walking across the ice as though he had spikes on his shoes. Badger shoots him a quick glare.

"I'd rather have a horse," Badger replies. "My boots make more sense when I'm on the back of a horse."

Eliyah stops at the far edge, grinning from ear to ear as he waits for his friend. Badger slips and falls again. The young cowboy is tempted to crawl across the ice like a baby. But he stands up, takes three more big steps, and lunges for the edge like a boy instead.

Makin' fun of my boots, Badger thinks with a grimace. *I'm hungry and my stomach's been flippin' somersaults since I ate Percy's awful breakfast. I'm cold, and my boots have to thaw before they can dry. I can't even feel my feet!*

"Eliyah, we have a bunch of strong, angry guys chasin' us. If they catch us, they'll kill us," Badger says. "How can you possibly be happy enough to smile?"

"The mob has not caught us yet," Eliyah says. "That makes you happy, right? We better keep moving though. I want to stay happy."

Badger trots up the side of the narrow valley, following Eliyah's effortless strides out of the canyon. After about a quarter-mile on the trail, they reach a sagebrush-covered plain. At first glance, the wide plain looks as flat as a dance-hall floor. As they walk, though, they realize it has many dips and draws.

"I think Nikos did it," Badger says.

"Why is that?" Eliyah asks.

"If he frames you for murder and it sticks, then you are gone and he can get jobs for his community."

"It would be a lot easier to frame me for stealing," Eliyah says. "I would be just as gone, and the foreman would still be alive to hire his men."

"Well, yeah, but …" Badger has no response. Eliyah's point makes perfect sense. The tired teen is sure Nikos pushed Mr. Churchman in, but he needs to get his argument right. If he can't convince Eliyah, he certainly won't be able to convince the sheriff.

At the top of the ridge, Badger looks at the sun almost directly overhead. He takes a deep breath and asks, "Whattaya think about Mr. Schmitz's story?"

"You mean the story about Win Churchman owing gambling debt to people?" Eliyah asks.

"Yes. If Mr. Schmitz is lyin' and he owed money to Mr. Churchman, then he might want the foreman dead," Badger says as the two continue their trek.

Eliyah shakes his head in disagreement.

"I have worked with Rolf Schmitz for nearly two years. Rolf is the most honest person I know."

"So if he is tellin' the truth, then Mr. Churchman owed money to Mr. Schmitz," Badger says. "So maybe Mr. Schmitz pushed Mr. Churchman in because he wouldn't pay the money."

"I know that is not true," Eliyah says, halting abruptly. "Rolf would not say boo to a goose. Rolf is a good man, Badger. Why do you say such bad things about him?"

"I don't really know him," Badger says, "but I do know you, and I'm pretty sure you didn't do it. And I know I didn't do it. But somebody did. If we don't figure out who, then we could go to jail—or worse—for a crime we didn't commit."

Eliyah is silent as Badger's words hang in the air like a stale horse fart. Eliyah sighs and rubs his eyebrows. He looks back in the direction of the worksite, and the two begin heading east again.

"I know what we have to do," Eliyah says.

"What's that?" Badger asks.

"First, we need to catch up with the mule train," Eliyah says. "Then I need to turn myself in."

"I would rather we talk to the sheriff after we have some clue that proves Nikos killed Mr. Churchman," Badger says.

The two friends turn a bit to the north so they will eventually cross the road between the worksite and Rogerson. *I hope we can catch the mule train,* Badger thinks. *It's our only chance to grab the train to Twin Falls.*

72

THE MULE TRAIN CHUGS east. A hill behind it blocks the dam from sight, and the village of Rogerson stretches out in front of it. Badger and Eliyah spot it as they approach from the south.

"Do we need to run to catch up with the mule train?" Badger asks.

"It moves slowly. We will catch it," Eliyah says.

Mule train is the strange name for the vehicle Badger and Eliyah are chasing. It is not a railroad train; instead, it is five wagons hitched together. A series of mule teams could pull a wagon train like this one, but a steam-powered tractor has replaced the mules. The giant tractor belches smoke from its boiler, and steam escapes with every move. The giant steel wheels have spikes that dig into the frozen dirt and move the train forward. The mule train brings cement and supplies from the railroad station in Rogerson seven miles to the dam worksite.

Badger feels small in this wide-open plain. He can see fifty miles in front of him, and there isn't a single tree. Sagebrush carpets the gently rolling hills.

Badger and Eliyah overtake the mule train and walk next to the engine. They wave their arms to draw the engineer's attention.

"Can we hitch a ride?" Eliyah asks.

"Sure, but we can't stop," the engineer says.

Badger puts his foot on a side rail, bounces twice, and swings onto the wagon. He struggles over the edge and flops in with a thud. With much

less effort, Eliyah climbs into the moving wagon.

Badger and Eliyah huddle in the front corner of the first wagon, which is about half full of coal used to fuel the burner that generates the steam to

74

power the tractor. The other four wagons are empty except for cement dust lining the boards. Badger is cold inside his frozen boots.

The engineer wears a thick coat and wool pants and sits in the tractor's seat. The mule train groans and clanks like a Pennsylvania steel factory as the giant wheels move the train forward.

A fireman jumps into the wagon with Badger and Eliyah. His blue coveralls are powdered black from the coal. His red cheeks are smudged black, and his brown gloves are blackened in spots as well. He scrapes a few lumps of coal into the bucket he is carrying. He will climb back into the tractor and shovel the coal into the burner to create more steam. The pressure from the steam will continue to push the pistons back and forth, and those pistons will continue to turn the wheels.

"Are you the last of the Bulgarians?" the man asks as he sweeps together more coal.

"You could say that," Eliyah says.

Badger smiles but remains silent. He doesn't look like a Bulgarian, but in an area where everyone is looking for a big Bulgarian and a local teen, two Bulgarians leaving the worksite isn't as suspicious.

The fireman looks up from his work. "There's been a steady stream of folks leavin' the past two days. On Monday, we picked up just one fellow—a little guy who had the personality of a grizzly bear. Since then we've had close to fifty guys ridin' to Rogerson. If I were smart, I would charge two dollars a ride."

A little guy on Monday, Badger thinks. *That*

might be Mr. Churchman's killer!

Badger makes eye contact with Eliyah. He nods toward the fireman, hoping Eliyah will ask about the little man. Eliyah grins at Badger but says nothing.

"Who was the first man to leave here?" Badger asks in an accented voice too deep to be comfortable. He doesn't sound Bulgarian; but he doesn't sound like a cowboy either.
Eliyah shoots Badger a curious glance.

The fireman, who doesn't know how a Bulgarian should sound, looks up. "He was dressed kinda nice in brown pants and shirt. Didn't look like a laborer; maybe an engineer."

"An insurance agent?" Badger asks, using his deep-throated accent.

"No, no, I remember the agent," the fireman says. "He came through last week on the mail stage. No, this guy on Monday was different."

Badger scratches his head. *Who could it have been?* he wonders.

BADGER AND ELIYAH SWITCH to a railroad train in Rogerson for the hourlong ride to Twin Falls. Sitting in his seat, Badger feels his last two nickels rub together in his pocket. *I'm glad Eliyah had a few extra coins to buy my train ticket,* Badger thinks.

The train is slow and wobbles from side to side, jerking uncomfortably forward. This passenger train is covered and moves faster than the mule train, but the drafty car they're in is colder than an icebox.

The train crosses the final bridge into Twin Falls, which is a new town. It doesn't have tents like in a boomtown; instead, new buildings are being erected everywhere. Made from bricks and stones, the structures are impressive.

As the train slows, Badger looks at Eliyah. "I can't believe you didn't ask the fireman anythin'. I had to use my stupid Bulgarian accent."

"Is that what that noise was?" Eliyah laughs. "You sounded like a bumblebee had stung your throat."

"If you would have asked about the guy, I wouldn't have had to," Badger says.

"My mind does not work like a detective," Eliyah says as the train stops. "If I get put in jail, Badger, would you find out who killed Mr. Churchman?"

"I would look for somethin' to prove you didn't do it," Badger says, "but I'm gonna be sittin' next to you in a jail cell. With Nikos leadin' a lynch mob, it's too dangerous on the outside."

As they shuffle down the aisle, Eliyah says, "I have a plan that will give you a chance to look for evidence."

"What's your plan?" Badger asks.

"It is a surprise," Eliyah says as they step down to the platform.

"I don't like surprises," Badger says.

"I do not like the cold," Eliyah replies, pulling his coat closer. "I hope the sheriff's office has a hot stove."

"And a hot meal," Badger says hopefully. "I'd be happy to go to jail for a hot meal."

THE JAIL IS INSIDE the new Twin Falls County Courthouse, which is made of giant granite stones. The front of the building has six huge granite columns, spaced evenly on either side of the door. They rise almost the full height of the three-story building. The courthouse looks like a Greek Parthenon in the desert.

Badger and Eliyah slow as their eyes scale the courthouse. They climb its majestic steps and stop. Even though they are anxious to get warm, they are nervous about going inside. Finally, Eliyah opens the door like a doorman at a fancy hotel and motions for Badger to step through. Eliyah follows, and they trudge down a marble-floored hallway. The hall is surprisingly light and warm.

A sign that reads *Sheriff* hangs from the ceiling above a door leading to an office. Eliyah hurries inside and stops in the doorway, his massive bulk hiding Badger from the sheriff's view.

"My name is Eliyah Dobrev. I am turning myself in for killing Win Churchman," Eliyah says.

"I'm Badger Thurston," Badger says, poking his head around Eliyah, "and I'm—"

"He is a witness to my crime," Eliyah interrupts.

Sheriff Jones stands and gestures for the two to sit. The lawman wears a leather coat with brown fur on the inside. His gray hat is new and small. He wears two pearl-handled pistols, one on each hip, and a shiny silver badge on his lapel.

"I got a wire about your crime. You two are makin' my job easy. I got caught up with an investigation here and, to be honest, I wasn't excited about headin' to Salmon Dam. Let me go get some paper so you can write out your confession and your statement," Sheriff Jones says, nodding first to Eliyah and then Badger.

"What are you doin'?" Badger whispers to Eliyah while the sheriff is away. "I wanna turn myself in too. Nikos wants to kill me!"

"If I confess to everything, the mob will not come after you," Eliyah says quickly. "That means you can go home, run away, or search for clues to help me. I cannot think like a detective, but your mind works that way, Badger. Please figure out who killed Win Churchman, so I can leave here a free man."

"How?"

Eliyah shrugs as Sheriff Jones returns with the paper.

Badger sits next to Eliyah and stares at the fancy gray-and-red patterns on the floor. *I can't return to the dam, or Nikos will string me up for sure,* Badger thinks. *What does Eliyah think I can I find out here?*

Chapter Seven

BADGER GRABS THE MAHOGANY RAILING as he climbs the marble steps inside the courthouse. The Twin Falls Public Library is on the building's third floor. A sign that reads *Library* hangs from the ceiling on Badger's right. The teen steps inside and shuffles to the reference section.

He grabs a cloth-bound book that lists all the businesses in Twin Falls and their locations. Badger's finger slides down the page as he scans for insurance agencies. He finds three. The cowboy-turned-detective scribbles their names and addresses on a piece of paper and shoves it in his pocket.

Badger looks at the wall clock. It is about a quarter past four, and most businesses close at five o'clock. With a gasp, he trots down the stairs and out the front door. The cold air hits Badger like a tidal wave. The day started off cold and has only gotten colder. The closest agency is on Third Avenue, a block away. The small white building has two windows and a plain front door. A tin chimney oozes gray smoke out the top. Badger scurries through the front door and steals some of the room's heat.

"Can I help you with somethin', young man?" an agent in a well-worn gray suit asks.

"I, um, well, you see," Badger fumbles. He hasn't given any thought to how to ask for the information he needs. He unbuttons his coat and sits on a stool in front of the desk the man is perched behind.

"Uh, I'm with the canal company out in Rogerson," Badger lies. "We had an accident, and someone died. The guy who croaked recently took out an insurance policy, and we need to notify the person who gets the money."

"You mean the beneficiary," the man says.

"Yeah, the beneficiary," Badger says, hoping to use the word with the next agent.

"I haven't sold any policies to anyone south of town," the man says. "I bet you want Donald Benson with the Carter Insurance Agency. He was just complainin' about a trip to Rogerson. He's two blocks down on your left, but he always leaves early on Wednesdays."

"Thank you for your help," Badger says abruptly as he jumps off his stool and rushes outside. Badger scoots down the stairs and races down the street as quick as a snowshoe rabbit.

AS BADGER APPROACHES THE Carter Insurance Agency, he slows and sucks in air to calm his rapid breathing. The building's design mirrors the other agency's. But this one is painted yellow. Its windows are dark, and the same style of chimney no longer smokes.

Badger bounds inside. A man in a well-worn blue suit is putting on his hat and coat.

"Sorry, son, we're closed," the man says gruffly.

"I just have a quick question," Badger says.

"Well, ask quickly then, because I'm leavin'," the agent says.

"Okay, Mr. …" Badger pauses.

"Mr. Benson, Donald Benson," the agent replies, "and time is wastin'."

"I work for the canal company in Rogerson," Badger says. "Mr. Churchman was killed at our worksite. He has an insurance policy, and we need to see who the bene—, benefi— Who gets the money."

"The beneficiary," the agent says. "And who are you to ask?"

"I'm with the canal company," Badger insists.

"What authority do you have?" the agent asks.

"I am, well," Badger flounders. The young cowboy is covered in filth, and a foul stench floats off him. He looks like a hobo. Badger realizes the agent isn't buying his story. "I work there."

"You work there," the agent says. "Well,

that information is private, and I need to see a death certificate before I can share it with you."

"But I just need—"

"You just need to get outta my office," the agent interrupts, pushing past Badger and out the door.

Badger steps into the cold. He cringes, and goose bumps pop up all over his body. The agent pulls out his keys and hunches to lock the door.

"It wouldn't take much time," Badger begs. "If you could just help me."

The agent straightens, turns, and glares at Badger. "Now listen here, kid. I'm late for my Wednesday night card game. Even if I wanted to help you, which I don't, I'm outta time." He turns his back on Badger and hurries away.

Badger shudders as the sun drops toward the horizon. His stomach twists into a knot. Percy's gross pocket biscuits are long gone, and Badger is both very hungry and very cold. Fear races through his belly. *If I don't find a warm place,* Badger thinks, *I'll be a popsicle by mornin'. Maybe I should join Eliyah in a warm cell. He won't get a great meal, but at least he'll get somethin'.*

Badger shakes his head. He doesn't want to die out in the cold, but getting out of jail would be far more difficult than getting into it.

BADGER KNOWS SOMETHING IN the back of his frozen brain, but he can't figure out what. He runs the conversation with Mr. Benson through his mind. The agent told Badger he needed a death certificate. Then the agent ordered him out and left.

Badger sits on the agency's bottom porch step and watches the brief encounter play in his head. They talk inside and step outside. Mr. Benson starts to lock the door. Badger interrupts him, the agent tells him no again, and the agent leaves.

Wait a minute, Badger thinks, relieved to know what's been tickling his brain. *He never locked the door!*

Badger hurries up the stairs and twists the doorknob. The door opens a crack. Badger checks the street for potential witnesses, but no one is lingering out in the bitter cold. He swiftly slips inside.

I can't believe my good luck! My detective abilities would really impress Eliyah.

Badger scurries to the pot-bellied stove in the corner and opens its big, rounded door. Peering inside, he sees a tiny glowing spark. Badger adds five sticks of wood from a pile next to the stove. He blows on the glowing ember, and a flame flickers to life. Badger blows twice more, and the flame leaps and dances inside the stove.

Badger huddles close to the stove and enjoys the heat. He removes his gloves and rubs his palms together as feeling returns to his hands. Badger's feet are still numb and tingling, but his groaning stomach demands his attention.

Badger searches the two cluttered desks. Finding no food, Badger rummages through the trash can. Near the bottom, he uncovers a stale loaf of bread. Badger's mouth waters. He lifts the rock-hard loaf out of the garbage and wipes some pencil shavings and lint off its top. Badger flips the bread over. The bottom is fuzzy with mold. It looks like it has a green beard. Badger is disgusted, but he is more hungry than he is grossed out.

Badger picks at the loaf, carefully pulling off all the mold. His stomach bubbles and groans, urging him to work faster. *Trust me, stomach,* Badger thinks. *It will be worth the wait.*

Satisfied with his efforts, Badger opens his mouth and presses the small loaf to his lips. The bread is too hard to break with his front teeth, so Badger pushes the bread to his canines. His teeth hurt as he crunches down to yank off a piece. He chews and chews and chews some more. He chokes as he swallows.

Badger looks around frantically for something to drink. A half-empty cup of cold coffee sits on one desk. Badger gulps a drink to wash down the bread. Cold coffee tastes even worse than hot coffee. But it goes very well with stale, moldy bread.

Badger struggles to finish his meal and then adds wood to the stove like it is someone else's job to chop the firewood. The little stove stays hot. For the first time in days, Badger is warm and his belly is full. He pulls off his boots and his outside layer of socks. *I hope they dry by mornin',* Badger thinks. A wool blanket hangs on a chair back. Badger wraps it around himself and falls asleep next to the fire.

BADGER STARES AT HIS CARDS. He has four

jacks and an ace. It is a nearly unbeatable hand.
Only four kings or four queens could beat him—or
a straight or a flush.

Three other men—a gambler, a miner, and
the saloon's janitor—carefully hide their cards.
Badger pushes the rest of his money into the middle
of the table.

"I'll call," Badger says to equal the
gambler's bet.

"That's too rich for me," the janitor says as
he lays down his cards.

The miner slams his cards on the table
without speaking. He's out of the game.

"Looks like it's just you and me," the
gambler says as he glances at Badger between the
brim of his hat and the top of his cards.

Badger glances back and tries to keep a
poker face. He looks at the pile of loot—almost a
dozen stacks of dollar bills, about fifty coins, three
mine claims, a horseshoe, thirty-two blue beads, a
pocket watch, and two dozen sausages. If he were
to win this hand, he could buy that white cowboy
hat. Nettie McCorkle would notice him for sure with
a fancy new hat. For tonight, though, Badger most
wants the two dozen sausages.

"I called," Badger says. "Show me your
hand."

The gambler places his cards down one
at a time—king of hearts, king of spades, king of
diamonds, two of spades. He pauses. If the last card
is anything other than the king of clubs, Badger
wins.

Badger holds his breath and his whole body shivers with excitement. Wait. That's not excitement; it's a cold shiver. "Someone should stoke the fire," he calls out. "I'm cold."

No one moves, so Badger, in a louder voice, says—

"Stoke the fire," and he opens one eye.

The stove no longer glows. Badger pulls the blanket up to his chin. He tries to go back to sleep, but it is too cold.

"Stupid dream," Badger says to no one. "And stupid stove."

Badger gets up and adds wood to the fire. It leaps to life, and the small building begins to warm again. Badger lights a candle, and his eyes adjust to the glow. Since he is awake, Badger decides to look for the insurance policy so he can see who benefits from Mr. Churchman's death.

To Badger's relief, Mr. Benson is organized. He has four desk drawers, and each houses the paperwork for the policies. In the top left drawer are policies for people whose last names start with A, then B, and so on. Halfway through the Cs, Badger finds a page that reads, *Churchman, James Winchester.*

Winchester, Badger thinks. *That has to be Win Churchman.*

Badger skims the policy. The text is confusing, and Badger barely recognizes it as English. Every sentence begins with *whereas or therefore.*

About halfway down the page, Badger sees

the word *beneficiary.*

Bingo, Badger thinks.

Just below *beneficiary* is the name Jean Churchman.

That could be Mr. Churchman's wife or mother or daughter or sister. Badger is stumped. *If the person who gets the insurance money is the most likely suspect, then why did Mr. Churchman's family member want him dead?*

The warmth is making Badger as tired as a barn cat in a ray of sunshine. *Maybe I will find the answer in a dream,* Badger thinks. He curls up in the blanket and falls asleep

Chapter Eight

BADGER WAKES TO A RUSTLING at the front door. A key is rattling in the doorknob. The stove fire is out, but the room is still comfortable. *I think I'll sleep in this mornin',* Badger thinks. *No! Get up, you fool!*

Badger jumps out of his blanket like a fireman when the alarm bell rings and slides into his boots and coat, shoving his extra socks into his pocket. He slinks to the front door and stands on the hinge side. Badger holds his breath as the door slowly opens, hiding him behind it. The insurance agent steps in cautiously and looks around.

Mr. Benson starts to close the door, so Badger grabs the door's edge and yanks the knob out of the agent's hand. Badger ducks under Mr. Benson's arm and bolts out the door. The cowboy feels his coat tug as the agent grabs it. Badger squirms in panic, and the coat slips out of the agent's fingers. Badger jumps off the porch without touching a single stair and hits the dirt running.

The teen runs as fast as he can. Badger normally wouldn't win a footrace, but he runs scared faster than the agent runs angry.

The agent yells, "Stop! Someone stop that boy!"

But no one hears. The cold has chased everyone inside.

Badger cuts through a vacant lot and runs through a half-built store on the opposite side of the block on his way back to the courthouse. The agent stops chasing after him. Badger slows to a jog. When the agent is out of sight, Badger drops to a walk and catches his breath. The cold air hurts his lungs, and Badger is sweating. The sweat freezes, and Badger begins fighting off a chill again.

I hope Eliyah can figure out why Mr. Churchman's family member wanted him dead, Badger thinks. *Because it sure doesn't make any sense to me.*

BADGER IS SHUDDERING WITH COLD beside the courthouse when the door is unlocked. Badger quickly slides inside, hurries down the hallway, and bursts into the sheriff's office.

Sheriff Jones sits at his desk with a steaming plate half full of eggs and sausage in front of him. He belches and rubs his stomach.

"I need to see Eliyah Dobrev," Badger says.

"You caught us in the middle of breakfast,"

the sheriff says before wiping his mouth.

"That's fine," Badger says. "I haven't had breakfast yet."

"Well, the county doesn't buy breakfast for presumptuous visitors," the sheriff says, "but the cook brought enough for a whole cell block, and the Bulgarian is the only inmate. I'd rather feed you than feed the pigs, so grab a plate."

"Thank you, sheriff," Badger says as he picks up a tin plate from a pile next to the steaming food and ladles on generous portions. He doesn't even sit down before shoveling forkfuls of eggs into his mouth.

"Do you wanna see the Bulgarian while you eat?" the sheriff asks.

"Yes, please," Badger says around a mouthful of sausage. "I'll go back and talk to him, if that's okay."

Sheriff Jones nods.

Carrying his plate, Badger waltzes through a narrow hallway that leads to a few steel-barred squares in the back. Badger has the manners of a wallowing pig as he shovels in a bite with every other step.
Eliyah sits on a bunk eating his breakfast.

"Mornin', Eliyah," Badger calls, speaking quickly. "I don't have long before the insurance agent heads this way to report me breakin' into his office."

"Get to it then. What did you find?" Eliyah asks.

"Well, it didn't make much sense and might

93

not help you."

Eliyah's smile wilts.

"A person named Jean Churchman gets the money," Badger continues. "Why would a family member kill Mr. Churchman? And who is she?"

"His wife," Eliyah says. "I remember Rolf talking about Mr. Churchman's wife, Jean."

"It just doesn't make any sense," Badger says. "She wouldn't kill him. She's not even around here, is she?"

"She lives in Pennsylvania. So Rolf said Win Churchman had a big gambling debt. And Jean Churchman gets the money from the insurance policy." Eliyah pauses and rubs his thinning hair. "It seems like Win Churchman had the most to gain from Win Churchman being dead."

"How's that?" Badger asks with an impatient glance down the hall.

"His gambling debt goes away, and his wife gets the money from the insurance," Eliyah says with a chuckle. "It is a pretty good way to make easy money."

"Except the bein' dead part," Badger says. "I wouldn't want that."

"You are right," Eliyah says. "It is almost a perfect plan."

Badger gasps. "Maybe it is the perfect plan!"

"What do you mean?" Eliyah asks.

"Maybe Mr. Churchman isn't dead," Badger says excitedly.

"That does not sound right," Eliyah says,

tipping his hat back and scratching his head. "I am in jail for his murder."

"That's the final piece of the puzzle!" Badger says, practically bouncing. "On his way out, he gets rid of his gamblin' debt and he gets an insurance payment for his wife."

"In Bulgaria, we call that 'one bullet, two rabbits,'" Eliyah says.

"In American, we call it 'killin' two birds with one stone,'" Badger says.

"You hunt birds with stones here? Why not use a gun?"

Badger grins. "I guess that doesn't make sense. But what does make sense is that Mr. Churchman gets his money and sends his biggest enemy to jail."

"I am Win Churchman's biggest enemy?" Eliyah asks. His eyebrows furrow, and he looks as confused as a gentleman who has just been slapped.

"I would say you are," Badger says. "He's leavin' his job with a lot of money, and you are sittin' here in jail with a lynch mob after you."

"But something fell in the concrete," Eliyah says. "I heard it."

"They never found a body!" Badger says, flailing his arms in excitement and sending a few crumbs of eggs tumbling to the floor. "It might be as simple as somebody throwin' in a rock and then Mr. Churchman's hat. It might've even been Mr. Churchman! Maybe you saw *him* runnin' away!"

"So if he is alive, where might he be?" Eliyah asks.

"Well, if Mr. Schmitz is right about his gamblin' debt, Mr. Churchman doesn't have much money unless he gets to his wife in Pennsylvania," Badger says. "And the best way to get back East is by rail."

"You better get over to the train depot," Eliyah says.

"It's been three days!"

"Maybe he hid out for a few days to let the excitement quiet down."

The cowboy-turned-detective suddenly hears stomping in the outer hallway.

"I bet that's the insurance agent," Badger says, and he bolts for the exit.

"Be careful, Badger!" Eliyah calls to the fleeing teen.

Badger tips his hat to the sheriff as he rushes through. He flings open the door and finds Mr. Benson reaching for the knob on the other side. The insurance agent's eyes bug out like a slimy frog, and his mouth falls open. Badger pushes past him and runs down the hallway.

"Stop that boy!" Mr. Benson finally yells down the empty hall.

THE TRAIN STATION IS a plain wooden building with a porch wrapped all around the outside of it. Its white boards are freshly painted, and the building feels new. Inside the station, a giant clock hangs above the ticket office. It reads half past eight. Badger's lungs burn from the bitter chill. Badger can see the courthouse in the distance, and he quickly looks around for Sheriff Jones and Mr. Benson.

Badger saunters up to the ticket window. The young teller, dressed in a blue uniform with a red stripe down the leg, sits on a stool behind a steel-barred window. He is maybe twenty years old and has a slight build and a baby face. A blue cap mostly contains his curly red hair.

I'm lookin' for a guy who is leavin' town to get outta a gamblin' debt," Badger tells the man.

"I hate card cheats," The teller replies. "I can't play a game of cards at this station without someone skippin' out on a debt. I'd be happy to help you."

Am I the only one who doesn't have a gamblin' debt? Badger wonders.

"So he's about an inch shorter than me," Badger says, smiling his thanks. "His hair is brown and gray, and he's probably not wearin' a hat. His face is pointy, and his mouth is tight. He looks like he was weaned on a pickle."

The teller chuckles. "I think I know who you're talkin' about. A guy was in here yesterday— not a very friendly guy—and he bought a ticket for the eastbound train."

"That's him!" Badger says excitedly. "Did I miss him?"

"No, the train was in for repairs yesterday. His train leaves at ten till nine today," the teller says. "He should be comin' in any time."

"That's great news," Badger says with a grin.

"How are you gonna stop him?" the teller

asks as he clears some tickets off the counter.

"I'm not sure," Badger says.

"Let me know if I can help," the teller replies as he looks up from his papers and checks his pocket watch. The silver watch has a train engraved on the back and has lines instead of numbers spaced evenly around the front.

"Sure thing," Badger says as he wanders to a chair and sits. Badger is too cold to think. His mind usually works out a plan in moments, but this time, Badger is coming up blank.

The train chugs down the tracks from the west. It oozes smoke out of the smoke stack and belches steam. The train pops an idea into Badger's mind. It's not a great idea, but it's the only one he has. Badger scurries back to the ticket window.

"If I grab his ticket, could you make sure he can't buy another until the train leaves the station?" Badger asks.

"Yeah, I could fumble around here with his money and ticket for about three minutes," the teller says as he pulls out his pocket watch to check the time. "Any longer, and it might look a little suspicious."

"So at eight forty-seven, I'll grab the ticket and run," Badger says.

"But then what?" the teller asks. "The next train comes through this afternoon."

"Could you get the sheriff down here to arrest me?" Badger asks.

The teller recoils and laughs. "You wanna be arrested?"

"The sheriff is lookin' for me anyway, and that's the best way to get him down here to see Mr. Churchman," Badger says with a coy grin. "And the

TICKE
PRICE

POCATEL
SALT LAI
DENVE

jail has a great cook. The way I see it, it's the best chance I have for lunch."

"Okay, I'll give Sheriff Jones a quick call. He should be down here pretty fast," the teller says.

"Now let's see if Mr. Churchman shows up," Badger says.

BADGER LOOKS AT THE clock on the wall. It is eight forty-five. Mr. Churchman slinks into the train station and sits on a bench near the door. He wears a fake horse-hair mustache. Badger rolls his eyes at the feeble disguise. The mustache slips, so Mr. Churchman takes it off.

Badger pulls his hat down near his eyes to mask his face like an outlaw on the run. Badger is just another nameless, faceless worker to Mr. Churchman, but he still hides. The cowboy looks at the clock. It is eight forty-six. Badger has to wait one more minute.

After a painfully slow minute, the train conductor strides across the platform. "The train for Burley, Pocatello, Salt Lake City, and all points east departs in three minutes," the conductor says in a deep, loud voice. "Form a line on the platform, and have your tickets ready."

About ten men and a woman with three children form a line. Mr. Churchman is second in line and holds his ticket in his left hand.

Badger tiptoes to the line, stepping easily so the platform boards don't creak. As he reaches Mr. Churchman, the teen snatches the ticket and races away.

"Hey, kid!" Mr. Churchman yells. "Stop that kid! He has my ticket."

Badger runs inside the empty train station, dashes around some benches, and throws the ticket in the fire. Mr. Churchman hurries after him and sees the piece of paper flash, turn black, and disappear into gray ashes. He looks like a child watching his only penny fall down a storm drain.

"You idiot!" Mr. Churchman yells as his look of disbelief suddenly shifts to anger. "I needed that ticket."

"Sorry, Mr. Churchman," Badger says.

"I'm not Win Churchman," the man says. "I'm Jim Smith, a businessman from Denver." He glares at Badger.

"I'm happy to see you alive, Mr. Churchman," Badger says, taking two steps back to get out of striking distance.

Mr. Churchman's eyes are on fire as he stares at Badger. He shakes with anger. The foreman spins and stomps to the teller.

"That boy stole my ticket," he says angrily.

"I know," the teller replies. "I called Sheriff Jones. He'll be here in a few minutes."

"No! No, sheriff! I just need another ticket," Mr. Churchman spits out through his rage.

"You don't want the sheriff to put this thief in jail?" the teller asks as he looks at his pocket watch.

"I just want to get to Denver," Mr. Churchman says as he leans in close to the steel bars on the window. "Just give me a replacement ticket."

"I can only give you a replacement for a lost or stolen ticket," the teller says without looking up from his logbook.

Badger looks at the clock again. It is eight forty-nine. All the other passengers have boarded, and the train is ready to go.

"My ticket was stolen," Mr. Churchman repeats.

"Then you need the sheriff to fill out a stolen-property report."

"No. No, sheriff!" Mr. Churchman yells again. "Just give me another ticket. I'll pay for it."

"All aboard!" the conductor drones from the platform. The train steams and belches.

"Hurry!" Mr. Churchman shouts. "I have to be on that train."

"What's your hurry, Mr. Churchman?" Badger asks.

"I'm not Win Churchman," the foreman growls.

"Is Win short for Winchester?" Badger asks.

"My name is Jim Smith, and I need a ticket to Denver," he says to the teller.

We don't get many requests for Denver," the teller replies. "I'll have to look it up."

As the teller pulls out his book of rates, the locomotive belches out steam and black smoke. Levers clank and churn and the train lurches forward.

"Hurry!" Mr. Churchman bellows.

"You need to calm down," the teller says. "I

don't work well under pressure."

Badger looks at the clock. It reads ten till nine.

Badger smiles and says, "Right on schedule."

Mr. Churchman grabs Badger by his coat lapels and yells in his face, "You made me miss my train, you urchin!"

Mr. Churchman throws Badger to the ground in the otherwise empty station and stomps back to the teller.

"Give me a ticket. I can run to the train," Mr. Churchman hollers.

"Train's gone," the teller says. "The window is closed. But the sheriff is comin', and you can make a report to him."

"I don't want to see the sheriff," Mr. Churchman yells at the teller. "I just want to get to Denver."

"Too late," the teller says as he replaces the book under the counter. "The sheriff is here."

The teller nods at the door as Sheriff Jones steps inside. He shakes off the cold, loosens his coat, and walks to the excitement near the teller window.

"What seems to be the trouble here, Simon?" Sheriff Jones asks the teller.

"We've had at least one robbery, maybe two," Simon the teller says.

Badger steps forward and looks directly at the sheriff. "I think I committed a crime," Badger says. "I stole a train ticket from Mr. Churchman."

"My name is Jim Smith. I'm a businessman from Denver," Mr. Churchman lies.

"Win Churchman is dead, Badger," Sheriff Jones says. "Your friend Eliyah is in jail right now for his murder."

"No one was murdered," Badger says excitedly.

"Why would Win Churchman change his name and fake his death?" the sheriff asks.

"He has a big gamblin' debt back at the camp," Badger says, "at least that's what Mr. Schmitz said."

"That Rolf Schmitz is a dirty, lying card cheat!" Mr. Churchman yells.

The sheriff pivots his head toward Mr. Churchman and raises an eyebrow. "You know Rolf Schmitz? I thought you were a businessman from Denver. Is that your story, Mr. Smith?"

"I, um, well, I knew Rolf Schmitz in Denver," Mr. Churchman says. He can feel his lies tangle up like fishing line in a tackle box.

"Skippin' out on a gamblin' debt is pretty despicable, but it's not anythin' I can jail him for," the sheriff says.

"What about takin' out an insurance policy and then fakin' his own death?" Badger asks.

"Well, that's fraud," the sheriff says.

"I looked him up at the Carter Insurance Agency and found a life-insurance policy Mr. Churchman took out on himself about a week ago. He named his wife as the person who gets the money."

"How did you get into the Carter Insurance Agency?" the sheriff asks.

"The door was unlocked. I just walked in," Badger says. "You could get Mr. Benson to identify Mr. Churchman."

"But Mr. Smith here isn't waitin' around to collect any money," Sheriff Jones says, pointing at Mr. Churchman.

"He's not stoppin' at Denver," Badger says. "He's on his way to Pennsylvania, where his wife is—"

"And where the money would be sent," Sheriff Jones interrupts. The lawman pulls out his handcuffs and approaches the foreman. "Win Churchman, you are under arrest for fraud."

"But my name is Jim Smith," Mr. Churchman pleads.

"Tell it to the judge," Sheriff Jones says.

Mr. Churchman turns on his heel and runs toward the door. Sheriff Jones reaches out but just misses him. As the foreman flees, Badger puts his leg out in Mr. Churchman's path. The foreman turns his head to look for the sheriff, and his foot catches on Badger's leg. Mr. Churchman smacks into the floor like an under-filled sack of oats.

The sheriff grabs his left wrist and slaps a handcuff on it. In one motion, the sheriff has Mr. Churchman's other wrist in a handcuff.

"Innocent men don't usually run," the sheriff says. "Thanks for your help, Badger."

"Anytime," Badger says. He smiles at Sheriff Jones like a puppy grinning at his master.

"I'm glad you're in a helpful mood," Sheriff Jones says as he pushes Mr. Churchman toward the door, "because you're under arrest, and I don't have another set of handcuffs."

"Under arrest?" Badger asks. "What did I do?"

"Trespassin' when you broke into the Carter Insurance Agency and petty theft for stealin' the train ticket," the sheriff says.

"But the door was unlocked!" Badgers objects. "And burnin' the ticket was to stop a fugitive!"

"Both of your crimes are misdemeanors. I just need one night in my jail," the lawman says. "I'll give you three meals and a warm place to sleep."

Badger thinks about breakfast, and a big smile creeps across his face. He remembers the nice, warm stove in the corner of the jail, too, and his smile stretches a little wider.

"Lock me up," Badger says.

THE STEEL DOOR CLANKS BEHIND Badger. Mr. Churchman sits with his head bowed in the cell next to Badger's, and Eliyah shares Badger's cell.

"You've been cleared," Badger says, as he sits on a bunk. "Why don't you leave?"

"I am the reason you are in here," Eliyah says. "I will keep you company tonight. Besides, I think this is the best hotel in town. The beds are not soft, but the food is good and the stove stays warm."

"What about tomorrow?" Badger asks. "Will you go back to work on the dam?"

"No, Badger." Eliyah shifts in his seat. "I do

not want to keep looking over my shoulder to see what Nikos is up to, and all my people have left."

"But Nikos should be in jail with Mr. Churchman," Badger says. "I'm sure they worked together."

Mr. Churchman looks up. "What are you talking about, you idiot? Why would I work with Nikos? He hates me as much as he hates Eliyah."

"But I'm sure he had somethin' to do with this," Badger says.

"I'm afraid you're wrong, Sherlock," Mr. Churchman sneers. "Nikos might have taken advantage of the situation, but I certainly wasn't working with him."

"Well, I was kind of hopin' Nikos would end up in jail," Badger says, grimacing. "So where will you go now, Eliyah?"

His friend's eyes light up. "I hear they are building the world's tallest dam in Wyoming. What about you, Badger? Will you go back to the dam?"

"I'm not the smartest person," Badger says. "But I know where I'm not welcome. I don't wanna be anywhere near Nikos."

"So what will you do?" Eliyah asks.

"I'm a cowboy," Badger says as he puffs his chest out, "and I have a friend who needs help with his herd of steers."

"You mean Percy?" Eliyah asks.

"That's exactly who I mean," Badger says. "I owe him, and it's past time I start payin' up."

"That makes sense," Eliyah says. "After all, herding cows is what cowboys do."

Glossary

axle—A bar or shaft connecting the opposite wheels of a wagon.

blueprint—A designer's or architect's drawing of a planned building or structure.

cast-iron stove—A wood-burning appliance that is used to heat a room and for cooking.

chisel—A tool with a cutting edge at the end used to cut holes in rock.

cowhands—Another word for cowboy or cowgirl.

depression—A hole caused by an object pressing down into mud.

engineer—A person skilled in the art and science of building structures or machines.

flint—A very hard kind of rock that strikes a spark when it strikes steel, which helps to start a fire.

flush (in poker)—A hand of cards in which each card is from the same suit, either hearts, diamonds, spades, or clubs. It is a nearly unbeatable hand.

fraud—A cheater or a deceitful or tricky action.

gatehouse—A shed or dwelling that shelters a

headgate. A headgate opens, closes, or regulates a pipe with water.

haggard—Having the look of someone who is wasting away from some type of suffering.

icebox—A kitchen appliance that keeps food cool. It requires no electricity, but an ice block must be added to it daily. Refrigerators have replaced most iceboxes.

interrogates—Asking questions of someone to discover facts.

lynch mob—An unruly, angry group of people who inflict punishment on an accused, often by hanging the person, without using a court of law.

mahogany—A type of wood.

measured—To speak in calculated or well-thought-out terms.

mule train—A line of wagons mules pull. In this story, a steam-powered tractor has replaced the mules.

Parthenon—A famous temple dedicated to the Greek god Athena. The original Parthenon is located in Athens, Greece.

sorrel—A horse with a red coat, mane, and tail.

straight (in poker)—Five cards in sequence, or order. An example would be an ace, king, queen, jack, and ten.

three-pole fence—A fence made with wooden posts with three wooden poles fastened between the posts.

vigilantes—People who take on the responsibility of law enforcement without legal authority.

well-kempt—Neatly groomed or tidy.

From the author...

Badger Thurston and the Mud Pits is fiction. But aspects of this book are based on real history.

In the early 1900s, Congress passed the Carey Act, which allowed private investors to build large irrigation projects. In exchange, the federal government gave these investors the land to be irrigated. The investment company would then sell the land and water from the project to farmers. The Twin Falls–Salmon River Company was one such group of investors.

From 1908 to 1911, the Twin Falls–Salmon River Company constructed the most massive concrete arch dam in the world. The dam measured 233 feet high and 450 feet wide and was designed to irrigate 78,000 acres of desert farmland.

The early part of the twentieth century was also a time of massive immigration from Europe. Many of these immigrants came to the West for opportunity. These laborers helped tame the West.

Laborers came to America from Italy, Spain, Greece, Poland, Serbia, Montenegro, Scandinavia, and Bulgaria. The Bulgarians were the largest segment of the labor force for most of the project. Near the end of the project, a dispute between the Bulgarians and management surfaced, presumably over working conditions and pay. All forty-nine of the Bulgarians quit the project.

The project was not as successful as planned. Less water than anticipated was available, and Salmon Dam only irrigated 35,000 acres on the Salmon Tract.

Despite its failure to irrigate the entire tract, the project created several amenities that were central to the development of the area. Power lines that were installed to provide electricity to the project are still in use today. The railroad that was extended from Twin Falls to Rogerson created a vital transportation link for the miners and livestock producers in the area. And the dam itself provided the best crossing over Salmon Falls Creek Canyon, which was the primary transportation route for the mining boomtown of Jarbidge, Nevada.

The project was also a primary market for some of the farmers and ranchers in the area. In 1909, my great-great-grandfather was awarded the contract to supply beef to the workers on the project.

About the author...

Gus Brackett was raised on a working cattle ranch in the wide open spaces of Southwestern Idaho and Northeastern Nevada. He was on the back of a horse by the age of five and sold his first steer at the age of ten. Gus was enrolled in a one-room school house where he first started writing stories about cowboys.

As a boy, Gus listened to tall tales about early cowboys from Grandpa Noy Brackett, Uncle Rolly Patrick and Truman Clark. Gus was fascinated by these stories and started writing the Badger Thurston series in 2010 to chronicle these tales.

Gus currently lives and works on the same ranch where he was raised. He is the Chairman of the Board of the one room school where he first wrote cowboy stories. He lives in a little ranch house with his wife Kimberly, four children, and a barn full of horses, steers, dogs, cats, and chickens. He is still writing so look for other books in this series.

20059016R00069

Made in the USA
San Bernardino, CA
26 March 2015